Championship Ball

The Chip Hilton Sports Series

For more information on
Chip Hilton-related activities and to correspond
with other Chip fans, check the Internet at
www.chiphilton.com

Chip Hilton Sports Series
#2

Championship Ball

Coach Clair Bee

Updated by Randall and Cynthia Bee Farley

BROADMAN
&HOLMAN
PUBLISHERS

Nashville, Tennessee

0-8054-1815-6

Published by Broadman & Holman Publishers,
Nashville, Tennessee

Subject Heading: BASKETBALL—FICTION / YOUTH
Library of Congress Card Catalog Number: 98-28095

Library of Congress Cataloging-in-Publication Data
Bee, Clair.
   Championship ball / by Clair Bee ; edited by Cynthia
Bee Farley and Randall K. Farley.
        p.   cm. — (Chip Hilton sports series ; v. 2)
   Updated ed. of a work published in 1948.
   Summary: When a broken leg forces him off the high
school basketball squad, Chip Hilton faces the coming sea-
son with all odds against him as he attempts to help build
a winning team.
   ISBN 0-8054-1815-6 (alk. paper)
   [1. Basketball—Fiction. 2. Sportsmanship—Fiction.]
I. Farley, Cynthia Bee, 1952–   . II. Farley, Randall K.,
1952–   . III. Title. IV. Series: Bee, Clair. Chip Hilton
sports series ; v. 2.

PZ7.B38196Ch   1998
[Fic]—dc21   98-28095
                                                      CIP
                                                        AC

4 5 6 7 8 04 03 02 01 00

TO
SY LOBELLO
PATRIOT, STUDENT, ATHLETE

HE GAVE ALL HE HAD FOR HIS COUNTRY AND HIS TEAM

Sy Lobello was graduated from Long Island University in 1941 with a
bachelor of science degree. While a student at the university, he played
three years of varsity basketball and captained the team in 1940–41.
He was killed in the Battle of the Bulge, December 1944.

COACH CLAIR BEE, 1948

TO
ROBERT MONTGOMERY KNIGHT
WITH LOVE AND APPRECIATION

HUSBAND, FATHER, EDUCATOR, COACH, MENTOR, AND AUTHOR

Clair Bee's loyal friend, a coach, and an educator dedicated to demanding
the best of himself, his athletes, and others.
A true student and steward of the great game of basketball.

RANDY AND CINDY FARLEY, 1998

Contents

CONTENTS

Foreword

I CAN remember that in the early and midfifties when I was in junior high and high school, there was nothing more exciting, outside of actually playing a game, than reading one of the books from Coach Bee's Chip Hilton series. He wrote twenty-three books in all, and I bought and read each one of them during my student days. His books were about the three sports that I played—football, basketball, and baseball—and had the kind of characters in them that every young boy wanted to imagine that he was or could become.

No one person has ever contributed more to the game of basketball in the development of the fundamental skills, tactics, and strategies of the game than Clair Bee during his fifty years as a teacher of the sport. I strongly believe that the same can be said of his authorship of the Chip Hilton series.

The enjoyment that a young athlete can get from reading the Chip Hilton series is just as great today as it was for me more than forty years ago. The lessons that Clair Bee teaches through Chip Hilton and his exploits are the most meaningful and priceless examples of what is right and fair about life that I have ever read. I have the entire series in a glass case in my library at home. I spend a lot of hours browsing through those twenty-three books.

As a coach, I will always be indebted to Clair Bee for the many hours he spent helping me learn about the game of basketball. As a person, I owe an even greater debt to him for providing me with the most memorable reading of my youth through his series on Chip Hilton.

Bob Knight
HEAD BASKETBALL COACH, INDIANA UNIVERSITY

DURING THE summer of 1959 at the New York Military Academy, not only did I stare at the painting of the fictional folk hero—Chip Hilton—that was on the wall behind Coach Bee's dining room table, but I had the opportunity to read some of the Chip Hilton series. The books were extremely interesting and well written, using sports as a vehicle to build character. No one did that better than Clair Bee (although John R. Tunis came close). By that time, Bee's Chip Hilton books had become a classic series for youngsters. While Coach Bee was well known as one of the greatest coaches of all time, due to his strategy and competitiveness, I believe he thought he could help society and young people most by writing this series. In his eyes, it was his "calling" in the years following his college and professional coaching career.

From 1959 until his death, I visited with Coach Bee frequently at the New York Military Academy and at Kutsher's Sport Academy, which he directed. He certainly touched my life as a special friend. Not only does he still rank at the top of his profession as a basketball coach, but he now regains the peak as a writer of sports fiction. I am delighted the Chip Hilton Sports series has been redone to make it more appropriate for athletics today, without losing the deeper meaning of defining character. I encourage everyone to give these books as gifts to other young athletes so that Coach Bee's brilliant method of making sports come to life and of building character will continue.

Dean E. Smith
HEAD COACH (RETIRED), MEN'S BASKETBALL,
UNIVERSITY OF NORTH CAROLINA AT CHAPEL HILL

IT'S SOMETIMES difficult to figure out why we became who we became. Was it an influential teacher who steered you toward biology? A beloved grandparent who turned you into a machinist? A motorcycle accident that forced you into accounting?

All I know is that in my case the Chip Hilton books had something—no, a lot—to do with my becoming a sports journalist. At the very least, the books got me to sit down and read when others of my generation were watching television or otherwise goofing off; at most, they taught me many of life's lessons, about sports and sportsmanship, about coaches and coaching, about winning and losing.

Since writing and selling to *Sports Illustrated* a piece about Clair Bee that appeared in 1979, I've written hundreds of other articles, many of them cover stories about famous athletes like Michael Jordan, Magic Johnson, and Larry Bird; yet I'm still known, by and large, as the "guy who wrote the Chip Hilton story." I would safely say that still, two decades later, six months do not go by that I don't receive some kind of question about Clair and Chip.

As I leafed through one of the books recently, a memory came back to me from my days as a twelve-year-old Pop Warner football player in Mays Landing, New Jersey. A friend who shared my interest in the books had just thrown an opposing quarterback for a loss in a key game. As we walked back to the huddle, he put his arm on my shoulder pads and conjuring up a Hilton gang character, whispered, "Another jarring tackle by Biggie Cohen." No matter how old you get, you never forget something like that. Thank you, Clair Bee.

Jack McCallum
SENIOR WRITER, *SPORTS ILLUSTRATED*

CHAPTER 1

Who's a Quitter?

ROBERT "SPEED" MORRIS tapped the brakes of his well-polished, and mostly reliable, red Mustang. With a short screech of tires, the flashy fastback stopped squarely against the curb in front of the Sugar Bowl.

The crowd of boys on the sidewalk looked up and scattered in pretended fear, screaming and yelling, "Mario, you're a long way from the racetrack!"

Speed laughed and nudged the tall, blond boy sitting in the black bucket seat. "OK, partner," he said, "unload the body!"

William "Chip" Hilton grinned and swung open the door and eased his broken leg onto the curb. As he limped across the sidewalk, he was greeted.

"Hi ya, Chip!"

"Hey, Chip!"

"How's the leg?"

Hilton smiled, stopped and talked for a few minutes, and then swung on through the Sugar Bowl door. Crutches would have helped ease the weight on his leg, but that would have been too much—he just wouldn't do it! Doc Jones had finally consented to eliminating them, but Chip didn't know he had been kept off his feet an extra ten days because of his dislike for those same crutches.

"Well, if it isn't Chipper himself," yelled Petey Jackson delightedly, spilling half the cola he held in his skinny hand. "Hey! It's great to see you walking. The crew's all here!"

Petey Jackson was one of the friendliest guys in town. He was older than Chip and had left school before graduating several years earlier to go to work. He was a dedicated sports maven and extremely popular with the athletes and the other kids who hung out at the Sugar Bowl. When Chip had been injured, Petey had been one of the first to visit him at the hospital. When Chip had been concerned about his job at the Sugar Bowl because it meant so much in helping out at home, Petey had volunteered to take care of Chip's work and had been handling both jobs all during Hilton's absence.

Petey pumped Chip's arm and checked him out. "I don't know, seems pretty soft to me! Must weigh two hundred pounds. Looks taller too!" He pulled a laughing and protesting Hilton to the old scales Mr. Schroeder kept by the door. "Get on, big boy," he said. "We'll see." He dropped a coin in the slot and then feigned shocked surprise. "Only 170? Six-feet-two and only 170? What'd they feed you up at that health resort?"

Chip hung on to Petey's hand as they slapped and tugged at each other. It was sure good to be back.

WHO'S A QUITTER?

"So, how ya feelin'? When ya comin' back to the old routine?"

"It's up to the boss. Hope it's right away. Where is he, anyway?"

"At his desk in the storeroom, as usual. Go on back."

John Schroeder was the most popular business owner in Valley Falls and was intensely interested in the high school students. Through Schroeder's sincere effort, Petey had returned and completed his requirements for his diploma from Valley Falls High School. Clearly, his interest went beyond the needs of his pharmacy business, for he was financially secure and could have retired long ago if he had wanted. Many people said he had opened the Sugar Bowl adjoining the other store just so the high school kids would have a place to go. Others said he did it to keep the teenagers out of the pharmacy.

He looked up from his desk as Hilton opened the door, and his surprised expression quickly changed to an enthusiastic smile.

"Hello, Chip! Am I glad to see *you!* Come on in here and sit down. How are you feeling anyway?" Without waiting for an answer, he grabbed Hilton by the hand and led him over to the desk chair. "Boy, I'll bet you're glad to get out of the house again."

"I sure am, Mr. Schroeder. I want to thank you for coming up to see me and—"

"Now, now," broke in the kindly man, "think I wouldn't?"

"No, sir—but—Mr. Schroeder—Mom wanted me to thank you for keeping my pay going. I didn't deserve it."

John Schroeder walked over and draped an arm around Hilton's shoulder. "Now, listen to me, young man. If you hadn't deserved it, you wouldn't have gotten it. Understand?"

Chip smiled. "I'd like to get back to work if you still want me."

"Well, you don't think for a minute anyone could take your place, do you?" Mr. Schroeder declared. "Sure, you can come back to work—the sooner the better! Petey's been doing fine, but he probably has every corner in the place swept full of dust. As for some of those showcases out there, they look like they hadn't been washed for a week!"

"I'll start tonight then, if it's all right with you."

"Sure, start right in. Tonight's a good time."

Chip did all the cleaning in the drugstore and the Sugar Bowl. His work consisted of sweeping out the two stores, washing the big glass windows, polishing counters, recycling papers, stocking shelves, unpacking and checking supplies, and boxing shipments. It was a tough job, but it was vital to Chip because it still left him time to do his schoolwork and play sports.

John Schroeder closed both stores at eleven o'clock every night except Saturday, and Hilton often started cleaning before the doors were locked. There was only about an hour's cleaning work to be done at night. Chip was allowed to do his other duties at any time of the day that best fit his school schedule. Occasionally, Speed Morris, "Taps" Browning, or "Biggie" Cohen would join him in the storeroom and study. Later, they would help him close up.

Chip peered out the storeroom door. It was just like old times: the jukebox still rocked out the latest hits. Speed was sitting on the last chair at the counter, intently absorbed in Petey's latest coin-and-glass trick. The regular players dropped tokens in the video games. A few couples were sitting in booths, eating burgers and fries. Out front, Chip could see "Fats" Ohlsen gesturing in the middle of a small group. Everything was the same. Closing the door gently, he breathed a sigh of satisfaction and rejoined John Schroeder.

Although several days had passed since Valley Falls had defeated Steeltown for the state football championship of Section Two, the wannabe quarterbacks were still talking about the victory. They grouped in front of the Sugar Bowl every evening and second-guessed the strategy of the coaches and even the quarterbacking of Speed Morris—everyone's hero.

Tonight, big, blustering Joel "Fats" Ohlsen, a head taller than anyone present, held center stage. He had singled out Chip Hilton as his favorite target and was spouting aggressively.

"Well, we won without the *great Hilton,* didn't we? He thought the team would fall apart when he got hurt. Anyway, he deserved what he got—hanging out with Brandon Thomas after the Delford game!"

"Yeah!" agreed one of the boys surrounding Joel. "Yeah, can you imagine that? The janitor of the Sugar Bowl had to ride home in a fancy sports car. Why, he was the great Chip Hilton, the star, the captain, the big shot!"

"Too good to come home on the bus with the rest of the team," sniped Fats. "No wonder they had a wreck—Hilton probably talked Brandon to sleep, bragging about himself."

"Don't really see how you can blame Hilton for the wreck," ventured Donald "Wheels" Ferris. "Brandon was driving, after all."

"Speedin's more like it," said Bob Graham.

"*Well,* he won't drive that particular car very fast again—," Ed Shelton began.

"You mean what's left of it," continued Wheels. "His father said Brandon couldn't drive for a year—guess he's really mad!"

"Yes, Hilton fixed everything, didn't he?" sneered Ohlsen. "Nearly lost Valley Falls the championship, broke his leg, wrecked Brandon's sports car, got Brandon in trouble, and worried his poor mother sick. And all just because he wanted to be the conquering hero and come riding home ahead of the team."

"Is that so?" drawled a quiet voice.

Biggie Cohen, unnoticed before, moved from where he had been standing in the shadow of the wall that separated the drugstore from the Sugar Bowl. Now the big football tackle moved deliberately in front of Ohlsen. Placing his hands on his hips, Biggie looked straight into Joel's eyes. The other boys began to press back against the big glass window. Everything about Biggie expressed overpowering emotion.

"Is that so?" Biggie resolutely repeated, his black eyes glittering angrily.

Ohlsen grew red, stammered, and vainly tried to find words. "I—I—," he feebly began.

"I know," Biggie growled. "You're a great talker—behind somebody's back." He flashed forward. Before Fats could move, Biggie pressed him against the building.

"Leave Chip Hilton alone! Understand me, fat stuff?"

"Sure—sure, Biggie," squeaked Fats.

"OK, don't forget it!" Biggie disdainfully turned his back on Fats, took a few steps, and then whipped around to face him again. "In case you don't know it, moron, Chip had as much to do with the winning of that game as anyone. He figured out the scoring play that tied the game, and he got Rock to let Speed drop-kick the winning point."

WHO'S A QUITTER?

He turned to the others in the stilled group, moving his steely gaze to each boy's eyes. "You guys oughta be ashamed of yourselves. Chip plays his heart out in everything he does—and you know it!" His voice was cold and hard.

The group dispersed quickly. Biggie had completely spoiled Joel's verbal assault against Chip.

Joel Ohlsen and Wheels Ferris were almost home before a word was spoken. Suddenly Ohlsen blurted out, "I hate that guy!"

"Biggie?"

"Yeah, him and Hilton both. I'll get even with them if it takes me twenty years!"

Joel's father, Joel Palmer Ohlsen Sr., was one of the wealthiest men in Valley Falls. As long as anyone in the town could remember, J. P. Ohlsen had been a dominant figure in its growth and development. Everyone in Valley Falls knew the hard-working and enterprising man as "J. P." Tall, angular, and dictatorial, he ruled his business associates and his employees with a firm but fair hand.

J. P. had several business interests and was the president and main stockholder of the pottery, one of Valley Falls's chief enterprises. He was a civic leader, a Valley Falls High graduate, and a devoted sportsman. Joel Jr. was J. P.'s only son and his only weakness.

"Biggie's tough," Wheels offered hesitantly.

"Yeah?" snarled Joel. "Just wait and see, Wheels! The bigger they are, the harder they fall!"

"Think you can take Biggie?" persisted Wheels.

"You don't think I'm crazy enough to touch one of the town's idols, do you?"

"Don't know—guess you can whip Hilton though."

"Did it once; I'll do it again too!"

"But Hilton had a bad leg, didn't he?" prodded Wheels. Then he quickly asked, "What've you got against Hilton anyway? What'd he ever do to you, Joel?"

Joel snorted, "Plenty! Think I'm gonna forget who started calling me 'fat stuff'?"

"What's so serious about that? Man, Joel, you are fat!" Wheels chuckled dryly. "Anyway, that was in third grade, and everybody called you that. Besides, we all called each other all kinds of names. I still have mine."

"Yeah? Well, we're not talking about you! I didn't think it was funny then, and I don't think it's funny now. You better watch out how you talk, too!" Joel threatened. Ohlsen was in an ugly mood, and the two parted in silence.

Completely oblivious to the recent scene outside the drugstore, Chip had scarcely moved from his position at Mr. Schroeder's desk when Speed Morris barged through the storeroom door. He was closely followed by Taps Browning. Morris waved a book and exploded, "Hey, Chip! Listen to this story about President Eisenhower."

Chip, accustomed to Speed's dynamic and frequent enthusiasms, slowly turned his head toward Taps and cautiously winked one eye.

Unfazed by Chip's lack of interest, Morris continued, "Eisenhower went out for football at West Point and broke his leg." Shaking his head in a determined manner and enunciating each word slowly, he went on, "And then he became a cheerleader!"

"I don't think so!" retorted Chip, swinging his body around and easing his leg up on a chair. "Let's see!"

Chip's eyes were glued to the book, but before he had finished the first page, he was interrupted by Taps.

WHO'S A QUITTER?

"Hey!" Taps was standing over him, his head practically scraping the ceiling light, arms swinging like a windmill. "Hey, Chip! That gives me an idea! Why don't you apply to be the basketball manager? Greg Lewis moved—bet you'd get it!" Taps was excited.

"Me? A manager?" Chip laughed incredulously. "Get real!"

"What's the matter with that?" challenged Speed. Then without waiting for an answer, he continued with mock sarcasm, "Oh, the great Chip Hilton—why, he wouldn't think of being a manager. Eisenhower could be a cheerleader at West Point, but that's different—he was just an ordinary guy, after all!"

For a moment Chip's temper flared, and his gray eyes narrowed angrily. All the frustration that had gnawed at his heart as he sat in the bleachers during the final game of the recent football season came near to finding an outlet now in bitter words. He'd burned up inside just watching. Speed probably didn't realize how it felt to be forced from sports. Sitting on the bench was bad enough, but to an athlete the thought of a permanent grandstand seat was unbearable. Slowly regaining his composure, Chip ventured, "Well, I didn't mean it that way, but—"

"But what?" persisted Speed.

Chip's thoughts ran on. Speed was one of his best friends; he couldn't quarrel with Speed. He'd shared everything with him. They'd been classmates ever since they had started school. Just the same, how could he ask Coach Rockwell to make him manager?

He looked up and then grinned slowly. "But nothing."

"Well, what about it?" persisted Speed. "We gotta have you around some way!"

Chip raised himself to a standing position and thought it over. Maybe it wouldn't be too bad after all— might give him something to think about, if he got the job. At least he wouldn't sit in the bleachers. He could be near the action and his friends.

Shaking his head and eyeing Speed's eagerness, he sighed resignedly, "OK, Mr. Sports Agent! OK."

"You mean it?" Speed asked excitedly.

"Sure!"

"That's great," breathed Taps, who had been silent but watching the exchange between Chip and Speed with tremendous interest.

"OK, pal, take a letter!" Speed wasted no time. "To Coach Henry Rockwell, Valley Falls High School. Dear Coach—"

"Wait a minute," hesitated Chip. "Maybe 'Rock' won't want me around after what happened."

"Forget it! That's ancient history." Speed shook his head impatiently. "Never look over your shoulder, me lad," he quipped. "I'll take care of it!"

The next half-hour was a turmoil of suggestions, criticisms, and heated debate, but at last the letter was finished. Speed grabbed it from Chip's reluctant hand and dashed out. "Be right back, Chipper, soon as I mail this."

Pivoting quickly, he barged across the room, threw a fake shoulder block at a packing box and half-ran, half-fell through the door.

"He'll break his neck someday," Taps mused.

Chip rumpled his short, blond hair with both hands and rubbed his forehead, reflecting. *Speed always knows what he wants and goes after it. I wish I were more like that.*

Later, after the boys had taken him home, Chip pulled Speed's book from his backpack and continued reading.

WHO'S A QUITTER?

Eisenhower nearly lost his leg when he was a kid because of blood poisoning. He wouldn't let doctors amputate, and it got well. Then, just as Speed said, he hurt it again at the Point, and when the doctor told him he could never play football again, he became a cheerleader. He almost didn't graduate because of his leg.

The book was full of stories about other personalities. Most of the anecdotes centered on men and women who had succeeded in sports in spite of physical hardships and overwhelming odds. Other profiles highlighted individuals who had dedicated their lives in service to others.

Chip had heard about the great female runner Gail Devers but hadn't known the whole story. Yes, she'd captured the U.S. Olympic gold in the one-hundred-meter dash. What Chip now read about was her valiant triumph over Graves disease. Just two years before her Olympic win, Devers suffered through and conquered the debilitating illness, including vision loss and a physical deterioration that nearly prompted her doctors to amputate her foot!

Each testimony conveyed the special challenges and circumstances each person faced. The words *determination, attitude, belief,* and *persistence* were in nearly every story.

Roberto Clemente's story immediately caught his attention. The Pittsburgh Pirates All-Star was killed in a plane crash off the coast of Puerto Rico. An earthquake had struck Managua, Nicaragua, leaving 250,000 people homeless. Clemente cut short his Christmas holiday to organize his own relief effort. Authorities believed the sixteen thousand pounds of much-needed relief cargo shifted in flight and caused the plane to crash. Today, Roberto Clemente remains an international hero. The highest award in major league baseball for sportsmanship and community activism is given in his name.

CHAMPIONSHIP BALL

Chip's spirit was touched by Roberto Clemente's words: "Any time you have the opportunity to accomplish something and you don't, you are wasting your time on this earth."

He closed his eyes and let his thoughts wander back to the night of the accident. Doc Jones had come right away. He'd worked half the night setting the ankle. Everything had to be just right with Doc. Good old Doc. He could still hear him saying, "Bum leg, nothing—you wait! That leg will be as good as new in six months." What if he had to limp the rest of his life? Then he could hear Doc saying again, "You can do anything—anything you sincerely want to do."

Chip undressed slowly; he was exhausted. Getting back on the job and making up his schoolwork had tired him out. He had never dreamed how much the Sugar Bowl and Petey and Mr. Schroeder meant to him. Then, too, he had missed the school crowd that made its headquarters at the store.

Clicking off the light, he stretched out in bed, his mind full of thoughts about the letter to Coach Rockwell and its possibilities . . . his mother too . . . her love and hopes. She sure was no quitter!

Mary Hilton was so small and appeared so young she could have passed for Chip's older sister. Chip and his mother each had a straight nose, gray eyes, a small mouth with thin lips, and the same shade of unruly blond hair. More importantly, beneath the similar physical exteriors beat tenacious hearts tempered by compassion.

Every evening Chip would put both arms around his mother, pick her up, hold her close to his chest, and swing her around in a circle. Mrs. Hilton would struggle and pretend anger. "William Hilton," she would scold, "put me down this instant!"

Chip would let her down then and pretend to be terribly frightened.

"I'm sorry, Mom," he would say, and Mrs. Hilton would forgive him with a kiss. They both liked the little game; it was their special way of expressing their love for each other.

Mrs. Hilton worked steadfastly and planned carefully for Chip's future. She was determined he would earn a college education, always talking about the day he would enter State. Nothing he said could ever shake her resolve.

"Why, Chip," she would protest, "you owe *that* to your father. His greatest hope was that you would graduate from college."

Just last night they had talked about college again. "But, Mom," Chip had protested, "I'd rather finish high school and go straight to work. I don't think I could stand it if I had to sit on the sidelines or worse—not play again. My leg—" He had been silent for a moment. "Besides, you need me here at home."

His mother had stopped him then. "We've made out all right so far, Son; we'll get along all right when you go to college. Besides, in the long run, a college education will make a tremendous difference in your life. Think of it as an investment in the Hilton family future. We've stepped out on faith before. We'll do just fine doing the same again now, Chip. You'll see."

Photographs and Memories

CHIP CLOSED the scrapbook with a crisp snap, crushed the *Yellow Jacket* between his hands, and pushed back from the desk. Grasping the book, he hurled it across the room and glared at Morris.

"Manager of a basketball team! You fixed it, all right. I must have been crazy to let you talk me into *that!*"

Yes, Speed had fixed it. That day's *Yellow Jacket* had carried the story of Hilton's appointment as basketball manager. Speed had hurried over with the school paper right after school.

Morris closed the book he had been studying and carefully straightened up from his comfortable position on the couch.

"What's eating you now?" he challenged, his black eyes studying Chip's scowling face.

"Aw, nothing. I don't know."

"What do you mean, you don't know?"

"Oh, I don't know. All my life I've been dreaming of a scholarship at State. That would have taken care of a lot of my expenses. Maybe I could have worked and sent some money home to Mom too. They don't give scholarships to managers, you know."

"They don't give 'em to all athletes either. You talk like you're the only guy who ever had a broken leg. Most of them heal stronger than ever."

"Could be."

"Could be, nothing. It's true!"

"S'pose it doesn't? What then? You think I'm going up to State and let my mother struggle for four years?"

"So, you'll get a job. I'll have to work."

"But your father's a lawyer—"

Speed firmly interrupted, "My parents already told me they expect me to work while I'm in college. They did and said working really made them appreciate their education. Besides, they say it's good for my character. So, we'll both work!"

"Nope, I'm not going to waste four years. I'll get a job in the pottery. It's probably where I belong anyway."

"Look, Chip, college is nearly two years away. We've got this year and then our senior year before college. Let's forget about it until after graduation. OK?"

"Guess so. Well . . . " Chip gestured toward the scrapbook and the scattered clippings, "guess I'd better change this thing to a photo album."

"That leg's only gonna need a little rest and time. Quit complaining! Bet you're playing baseball by spring. Anyway, there's more to school than sports!"

"Coming from you, that's a good one!" exclaimed Chip, moving dejectedly toward the door where the scrapbook lay on the floor.

"Shoot!" shouted Speed, glancing at his watch. "I'm late for supper! Mom'll kill me!"

He grabbed his coat with one hand, petted the cat with the other, and dashed out the door. "Hate to leave you, bud, but I'm late already." Speed looked back over his shoulder and talked as he ran.

Chip watched Speed turn at the end of the hall and swing out the front door. Speed's footwork always amazed him, but this afternoon it struck home hard. Speed was the only player on the squad who gave him any competition when Coach Rockwell called for a race the length of the football field.

Speed would explode from the line at the sound of the gun and take the lead for the first fifty yards; then Chip's long strides would begin to tell, and he would slowly creep up and take the lead ten yards from the goal line—always close. It seemed as if he and Speed had always pushed each other.

Sitting at his desk, Chip read the clipping slowly and reflectively. He had cut the article from the sports page of the Valley Falls *Yellow Jacket*. He hadn't even thanked Speed for bringing the paper over.

Once more he looked at the clipping. By now he had almost memorized the contents:

Former Varsity Star Appointed Basketball Manager

William "Chip" Hilton, a member of the junior class and a star center on last year's basketball team, will serve as varsity basketball manager this year.

Hilton was injured several weeks ago in an automobile accident. He was co-captain of the football team and a great passer and kicker.

Hilton's injury keeps him out of a basketball uniform, but the team will be fortunate in having an experienced basketball player as manager.

Chip is the son of the famous William "Big Chip" Hilton, All-American football and basketball player, who played at Valley Falls High before going to State. Mr. Hilton, formerly chief chemist at the Valley Falls Pottery, was killed in an accident there several years ago.

Frank Watts and Herbert Holden were named assistant basketball managers.

Chip laid the heavy scrapbook on the desk at his side and pasted in the clipping. Somehow it looked insignificant among all those empty black pages he had hoped to fill with his junior year clippings. The fact that the first half of the book bulged with glowing accounts of his freshman and sophomore years only disheartened him. Headlines, and sometimes whole columns of type, told of his athletic feats and record-breaking accomplishments.

Turning the pages, he glanced at the headlines and relived every thrilling moment they recalled: "Valley Falls Wins, Chip Hilton Stars," "Hilton and Morris Selected for East-West All-Star Game," "Morris and Hilton Chosen All-State," "Hilton and Morris, Three-Letter Stars, Attend Spring Practice at State."

Hilton had earned six letters at Valley Falls High before his junior year. "Guess that's the end of that," he murmured.

A familiar stride on the front porch brought him out of his reverie. The door opened and in the dimly lit hall only Taps Browning's shoulders were visible. Then with a duck of his head he was in the family room. "Hi ya, manager," he beamed, waving a copy of the *Yellow Jacket* in the air. "See the paper?" Taps was exuberant. His blue eyes sparkled behind his glasses.

"Yes, I saw it. Speed brought it over."

"That's the best news that's been in the paper this year! How you feelin'?"

"OK—except for this manager stuff. Don't know whether that's good or not, Taps." Suddenly his mood changed, and with a wry grin he added, "Anyway, I guess I won't have to pay my way into the games."

Taps sensed Chip's feelings and said quickly, "You sure won't, Chip. Everybody's been pulling hard for you. The team needs someone like you. You'll be a help to all of us—especially me!" Grasping Chip gently by the arms he added, "I'm glad you're going to be manager, Chip. Maybe now I'll be able to make the team. I don't know what I'd do if you weren't around. It doesn't seem it was only this fall we met out there on the Hilton A. C. court, remember? You taught me more basketball—"

The tall youngster broke off suddenly to protect himself from a good-natured, though threatening, gesture from his friend.

"Cut the sob stuff, kid," growled Chip.

"Well, see you in the morning, Chip. I gotta stay home tonight. Mom and Dad said they wanted to see what I look like. Besides, Suzy's got some big news about a running club she's starting with some of her friends at school. 'Night!"

"Twenty-two, twenty-three, twenty-four."

Chip stopped counting and paused for a rest. This was hard. He breathed heavily and was glad he had reached the landing. Come to think of it, this was the first time he had been up the gymnasium steps since before the Steeltown football game.

How about that! He had never even noticed counting steps before. Now he bet he knew how many steps there were between every classroom and every floor in Valley Falls High School.

Chip sensed something distinctive in the air today. It was the approach of winter—that meant basketball. Yes, basketball was in the air! His pulse quickened.

He looked back down the long flight of steps. Funny, he had never realized before how many steps led to the gym. Glancing at the huge gym door, he started upward again, counting as he climbed: twenty-five, twenty-six, . . . twenty-nine, thirty. The big door required more effort to open than he remembered, and he was glad to find himself inside. He paused inside the big foyer, a bit out of breath, as he used to be after he'd dashed up these same steps, three at a time.

Arriving in front of Coach Rockwell's office, Chip stopped for a few seconds to collect his thoughts before knocking. He knew a lot about this office. Every inch of wall space was covered with pictures of the teams and great players who had played for Coach Rockwell and Valley Falls down through the years. His dad's picture was up there; maybe his would be there, too, someday. Right now, though, he was more concerned with his appointment with Coach Rockwell. Well, he'd better get it over with.

A hearty "Come in!" greeted his knock, and Chip found himself face to face with the coach. Chip stood there tongue-tied. In the hospital and even at the championship football game, when Coach Rockwell had asked him to sit up in the stands and help figure out the weakness in Steeltown's defense, he had tried unsuccessfully to work up enough nerve to unburden his feelings, to tell the Rock how sorry he was for breaking a team rule after the Delford game.

Chip had mentally rehearsed this meeting many times and practiced just what he would say. It wasn't because the Valley Falls head coach was someone to be afraid of or the kind of man a guy couldn't talk to freely. Not at all. In the many years Rockwell had taught football, basketball, baseball, and sportsmanship to successive generations of boys at Valley Falls High, he had become a town institution. A strict disciplinarian, he demanded the best a person had in him at all times. The guys on his teams grumbled over the long, extra hours of practice he required, but a Rockwell-coached athlete was welcomed on every college campus. Coach Henry Rockwell was a perfectionist.

The Rock knew and understood boys. He knew, for instance, what had been troubling Chip ever since the accident following the Delford game more than a month ago. He had no patience with team members who broke rules. He knew Chip had had a good reason. If only the teenager had told him why he had to get back to town early.

But he also knew Chip wouldn't betray a confidence. He had taken the consequences. And now the athlete was worried because he had put his coach in the position of showing favoritism to a player who had broken a rule. Well, the Rock understood loyalty and sensitivity. Coach Rockwell shook himself out of his contemplation and looked up.

"Why, hello, Chip. Come in. Sit down." Rockwell's face was friendly, and he smiled a little as he quizzed, "Been worrying about this little meeting?"

PHOTOGRAPHS AND MEMORIES

Chip was relieved by the friendly greeting, and all his uncertainty vanished. "Yes, I have, Coach. I've been wanting to tell you how sorry—sorry I am for the way things turned out. The team bus had already left, and the bus wasn't leaving for almost another two hours. I was standing outside the terminal wondering what to do, when Brandon pulled up next to me. He said he was going home and I could ride with him. I didn't mean to break the team rule."

"It's all right, Chip. OK?"

"Yes, but, Coach, I never planned to ride home with Brandon, and when he stopped at the inn, I waited in the car. After a while, I went in to get him. That didn't work, so I started walking—nobody I knew came by. Then Brandon stopped for me again. Not long after that there was a truck on the side of the road and a car—"

"Chip!" There was a note of finality in Rockwell's voice. "What's done is done!" He leaned back in his chair, and his friendly black eyes scanned the tall teenager. "I know just how you feel, Chip. Exactly how you feel. And I know the whole story, too, about that night you got a lift in Brandon's car. In your shoes and in the same situation, I probably would have done precisely as you did. What say we move beyond it and start all over in basketball, OK?"

Chip's throat was dry and his chest tight, but the deep breath he took cleared away the feeling. He managed a faint, "Sure, Coach."

The green leather chair squeaked a bit as Rockwell swung it toward the window and shifted his eyes out over Ohlsen Stadium. The room was quiet while Coach Rockwell's thoughts flew back over the years—to other years when another tall, blond youngster with level, gray eyes had sat in front of his desk. That boy was called Chip too.

Again the leather chair protested as Rockwell turned back to his desk. "Leg bother you much now?"

"No, sir, at least not too much."

"I'm glad to hear that! I saw Doc Jones yesterday, and he said it was coming along fine. Doc tells me he's fixing you up with one of his special braces tomorrow. That old guy knows more about bones than any big shot in the surgical profession. If he were located in some big city, he'd be a bone specialist in great demand. Here, to us, he's just old Doc Jones." The coach was silent for a moment. Then he nodded reassuringly and added, "It'll come along all right in time."

"I sure hope so," Chip declared earnestly. "I'd give anything to play one more year of football."

"You will, Chip. You've got a lot of football left."

Coach Rockwell spoke in such a friendly tone that for a moment Chip forgot himself. "I always dreamed of playing at State!"

Coach Rockwell broke in quickly. "You will, Chip. I wrote to State about you and Speed even before they had you up for their reception last spring."

The coach rubbed his clean-shaven chin and studied the tall youngster with keen eyes. "What courses are you taking?"

"College prep. The counselor, Mr. Lowman, said they would be the best courses for me, Coach."

"What are you going to study in college?"

"I was planning to go to State and study chemistry—" Chip stopped suddenly. He had nearly added, "if my leg is OK."

"Ceramics," queried Rockwell, "like your dad?"

"Yes," Chip finished faltering. "But I had journalism in mind too."

"What kind of journalism? News? Sports?"

"Sports, I guess. I like sports stories."

"No reason you shouldn't be anything you want to be, Chip—a ceramics chemist like your father, a sportswriter like Joe Kennedy or Pete Williams, or a physician like Doc Jones. But there's time for all that later. The main thing right now is doing your very best in high school." Then he added, smiling, "And really learning the great game of basketball."

Coach Rockwell moved quickly from his chair to a bookcase near the files. Glancing rapidly along a shelf, he grasped a black-bound book. "Here's a book you should read: Dr. James Naismith's *Basketball: Its Origin and Development*. Take it along and bring it back when you've finished." He paused a moment. "You'll get a lot of basketball out of that little book, no matter whether you plan to be a coach, a sportswriter, or whatever!"

Chip felt a glow of confidence now, and his heart beat rapidly as the coach went on, "Dr. Naismith's book will give you a good background for basketball, and it contains a lot of interesting information that's not generally known. The best place to start is at the beginning, and for basketball, Naismith is the beginning!"

"I hope I can do a good job as manager, Coach."

"You will. You've played the game, and you've had more responsibilities than most boys your age. By the way, will this manager's job interfere with your job at the Sugar Bowl?"

"Oh, no, sir. No, sir!"

"I'm glad of that. I know one thing for sure, Chip. If your dad were in your shoes, he'd be right in there pitching, giving all he had for the team, whether he was the star, a sub on the bench, or the manager!"

Pointing to the book Chip was holding, he continued, "The man who wrote that book and who invented basketball had the right spirit. Naismith showed a lot of courage when he went in for physical education and athletics. He had to buck everybody—his friends, his only sister, the church, and his teachers. But he felt, as do most coaches who love their work, no adult can have a better job than the opportunity to work with young people and help them develop into real men and women."

Chip was silent for a moment. Then, getting back to his own problem, he said hesitantly, "I don't know much about being a manager, Coach."

The corners of Coach Rockwell's thin lips twisted into a half-smile as he regarded the boy amusingly. "You didn't know much about football either, four or five years ago, did you, Chip?"

Chip smiled and scratched his head. "I sure didn't!" Suddenly he felt sure of himself and made a mental resolution. He'd be the best manager Valley Falls ever had. If Eisenhower and Clemente could dedicate themselves to others, then Chip Hilton could dedicate himself to being a manager—a good one!

CHAPTER 3

A Chip off the Old Block

DOWNSTAIRS IN the Hiltons' big living room, Speed, Biggie, "Red" Schwartz, and Ted Williams were singing. Mrs. Hilton was playing her favorites, and the boys were trying to sing in harmony but were off-key and generally having fun. Although Ross Montgomery never sang, Chip could visualize him sitting beside his mom on the piano bench, following the music. Pretty soon, when she got tired, Ross would take over.

Then the keys would really talk! Ross was talented and could play any type of music well. Chip guessed he liked his mother's playing best though. It seemed more homelike, more natural.

Chip was sitting in front of the computer, concentrating on the English paper that Mr. Wilkinson wanted at his next class. Naismith's book and the other book on basketball had provided some good material for the essay, and Chip had jotted down a number of facts he felt would be interesting.

Basketball was a natural. What else could he have put his heart into this evening? Nothing! Basketball was surging through his veins.

Chip made good marks in English, but it was always a struggle. His thoughts wandered away from his writing, and he began to think of his future. If he had trouble with a little English paper, how could he ever be a sportswriter?

Ross Montgomery was playing now, and suddenly the guys burst into a laughing, rapid rendition of "Old MacDonald's" tricky lyrics. Finally, this was a song they all knew, and the words rang out loud and clear—yet still off-key:

Old MacDonald had a farm, EE-YI, EE-YI, OH!
And on this farm he had some chicks, EE-YI, EE-YI, OH!
With a chick-chick here, a chick-chick there,
Here a chick, there a chick, everywhere a chick-chick,
Old MacDonald had a farm, EE-YI, EE-YI, OH!

Chip stopped working on his composition and listened intently. The melody was old and familiar, but some lyrics of his own ran through his mind in time with the music:

Old Chip Hilton has a leg, EE-YI, EE-YI, OH!
And on this leg he has a brace, EE-YI, EE-YI, OH!
With a limp-limp here, a limp-limp there,
Here a limp, there a limp, everywhere a limp-limp,
Old Chip Hilton has a limp, EE-YI, EE-YI, OH!

His thoughts turned suddenly to Doc Jones, and he imagined the words "Old Patch-'Em-Up" would have substituted:

A CHIP OFF THE OLD BLOCK

Old Chip Hilton has a brace, EE-YI, EE-YI, OH!
But someday this brace will go, EE-YI, EE-YI, OH!
And when it goes, he'll be aglow, EE-YI, EE-YI, OH!

Can't come too soon, Chip thought. *Here, how about "Wilkie's" composition?* He tried to concentrate on the paper again, but it was no use. Despite his very best intentions to study, his thoughts turned to the basketball team and the part he might play in its success. Greg Lewis had been manager for the past two years and had gone on the trips, kept score, and handed out the equipment. There seemed no way to be outstanding in that job?

Speed's friendly shout from the downstairs hallway broke his thoughts. "Hey, Chip! Come on down. What ya doing? Tomorrow's Saturday, and you can study all day."

"Wonder what kind of job he thinks I've got," Chip muttered. "OK," he called. "Be right down." He might as well go down with the guys; he couldn't concentrate with all that noise anyway.

The big, brightly decorated living room was crowded. Every chair and sofa—even the floor—was occupied. Everyone greeted Chip as he entered with, "Hi ya, kid!" and "Hello, manager."

Ross Montgomery sat at his usual place on the piano bench. "What'd Coach say?" he asked.

"Oh, he gave me a real going-over. Talked mostly about my job and then went into the career routine."

"He would!" Ted Williams laughed. Ted was president of the senior class. He was so shy and quiet it was hard to realize he was a star football player.

"The taskmaster!" grunted Red Schwartz.

Chip agreed mentally. Coach Rockwell *was* a taskmaster when it came to coaching, but the players all seemed to like it! He sure appreciated Rock's discipline, even that time last fall when the Rock had bawled him out.

"Ya see Rogers?" queried Red as he dipped his hand into the large popcorn bowl in the center of the coffee table.

"No," shrugged Chip. "I just talked to the coach."

"Rogers is the only man alive who can get one up on Rock," said Speed.

Burrell Rogers was the Valley Falls athletic director. However, he seldom concerned himself with coaching, confining his activities to administrative work.

"Who's really the boss—Rock or Rogers?" Soapy asked.

"Hah!" snorted Speed. "Nobody bosses Rock except the school board. Most of *them* are scared of him. Rock is a Valley Falls institution."

"I don't think he's very optimistic about this year's material," Chip said.

"Look," protested Speed. "Rock always uses that line. We won't have many guys out for the team this year, but so what?"

"Hampton'll have more out for their team than we have in the whole senior class," laughed Red.

"Well, Coach doesn't do so bad with what he gets," broke in Biggie. "He's won more championships than all the rest of the coaches in the state put together, I guess."

"He said the schedule was the toughest in the history of the school," said Chip.

"That's him, all right," laughed Red. "Always worrying. Rock waves the biggest crying towel in the state!"

"He's a great moaner," agreed Ross, securing himself more firmly on the piano bench, "but I can't see any need to cry about this year's basketball prospects. There's Red and Speed here, and who could forget our illustrious Soapy Smith, of course," Ross poked at the redheaded athlete, who responded with a deep bow. "And, there's Miguel Rodriguez and Chip's newest recruit, Taps—what more does he want?"

"It's sure surprising the interest some people we know show in sports," observed Chip, "even though they profess to doubt their value."

Ross stood up and shook his head ruefully. "I'd better go. I'm in a den of athletes!"

"I've got to go, too," said Speed, jumping from the floor abruptly. "Don't worry. We'll have a good team. We've got the best coach in the state, and the first All-State manager in the history of basketball."

"Hah!" grumbled Chip, clumping up the stairs to get his coat before leaving for the Sugar Bowl.

Chip paused outside the open door of Coach Rockwell's office. The Rock, Burrell Rogers, and Assistant Coach Chet Stewart were seated at the big table. Waiting uncertainly, Chip was relieved when Coach Rockwell looked up and greeted him with a smile. "Come in, Chip."

Chip entered the office and laid the books Rockwell had loaned him on the desk. "Here are your books, Coach. Thanks a lot. They were great!"

"Good! I'm glad you liked them."

Chip had never had much contact with Burrell Rogers, but Chet Stewart had been his backfield coach in football and had worked with Coach Rockwell in teaching him basketball for the past two years. Chip knew him well and liked him. He was thrilled at the thought of becoming a part of Valley Falls's board of basketball strategy.

"Sit down next to Chet," continued Coach Rockwell. "You two will have to work pretty close, you know."

Chip smiled. "Sure hope I can help," he said.

"We'll need a lot of help with the schedule Rogers pulled out of his hat for us this year." Rockwell was serious now. "It's a suicide schedule for a small squad, and it begins to look as if that's what we'll have."

"First team'll be all right, Coach," interrupted Chet Stewart.

"Not unless we find a center, Chet. A lot depends upon the new candidates. Especially Hilton's protégé, Browning." Coach Rockwell smiled at Chip. "If he only has half your fight, kid, he'll be OK!"

Chip suddenly felt a heavy sense of responsibility. *Speed was right,* he reflected. *He said this job was a tough one. Man, wouldn't it be great if Taps could make the team! Maybe I can help a little there, anyway . . . guess I know Taps better than anyone. He'll make this team or my name's not Hilton . . . glad he lives next door, handy to the Hilton A. C., his and my favorite spot. I'll always be grateful to Dad for putting up that backboard and hoop, the football goal posts, and the pitcher's rubber. Dad had wanted me to be a good athlete. I guess I know now how he felt. I feel the same way about Taps.*

"Maybe Browning will develop," Stewart said hopefully. "He's got everything a pivot player needs: height, long arms, and he's a pretty good jumper."

Rockwell laughed. "How do you know so much about him?"

It was Stewart's turn to smile. "I've been hearing about Hilton's find from every kid in class. Chip's been working with him in the Hilton backyard every day. I think Chip's got something!"

Rockwell sighed. "I hope so! We sure need a big man!" He stood up abruptly. "Let's see the game video."

A CHIP OFF THE OLD BLOCK

"Good," beamed Rogers. "Pop's got the Weston video all set."

Rogers led the way out of the office, and Chip hobbled along beside Chet Stewart. "How's Pop?" he asked.

"Pop? You know Pop—he's *always* all right. What a worker! Serves as the trainer, oversees the locker room, and does about everything ten other guys should do!"

"Say, how old is Pop?"

"Well, he's been here at Valley Falls for thirty-five years, but that doesn't mean much. Your guess is as good as mine."

Chet quickened his pace to catch up with Rogers and Rockwell. Chip tramped along after him.

The stiff formality of Rogers's office was in sharp contrast to the warmth and fellowship of the room they had just left. Pop smiled broadly as they entered the room. The little stoop-shouldered man was dressed carefully in a blue suit. *Wow! I never thought of it before, but Pop dresses better than Coach.*

"All set, Pop?" asked Rogers briskly.

"Yes, sir!" The old fellow smiled enthusiastically. "Rarin' to go!"

"All right, let's go."

The others seated themselves on the couches in the corner of the office. Pop started the tape in the VCR, and the men were carried back in time, right into last year's Weston game. Chip had played in that game—last year, a regular on the varsity—this year, a manager.

When the tape finished, Rockwell and Rogers said good-bye and filed out of the office, each busy with his own thoughts.

Chet Stewart stretched and then, grabbing Pop affectionately by the arm, said, "Pop, Chip's our new manager!"

"Yes, sir, I know that, Chet. Chip off the old block, Chipper is."

"Sure is," agreed Chet. "Say, I've got to go! Mind, Chip? See you Monday! Four o'clock!"

Chip helped Pop put away the game film, store the video equipment, and lock the office. This routine was all new to Chip—he hadn't realized all the duties managers were responsible for behind the scenes. Then they walked down the hall toward the gym lobby. Just before they reached the big door leading to the outside steps, Chip hesitated a moment and looked around. The big foyer was lined with cases containing trophies, plaques, stuffed and varnished footballs, basketballs, and row after row of baseballs—on display for all to see the Valley Falls victories and championships. Suddenly, Chip turned and limped over to a case that housed several lacquered basketballs. One ball in particular always held his interest.

"Bet I know what you're looking at, Chipper." Pop shuffled over to the trophy case, adding, "The basketball the team gave Big Chip!"

"That's right, Pop!"

"That basketball you're lookin' at," Pop continued, "was the first state championship ball Valley Falls ever won. Your pop won that championship practically by himself."

"It's really something when a team feels that way about a guy, isn't it?"

"Sure is!" Pop twisted his head a bit and asked, "Say, you had any more trouble with that no-good Fats guy?"

"No, Pop. Not lately."

"Well, Chipper, don't forget—I trained some mighty good fighters in my time, and I can fix you up. No foolin'."

Chip laughed, and before he realized it, he found himself back on street level. He didn't even remember limping down the steps. He was thinking about that championship basketball and the player who had done most to win it—his dad.

Mike Sorelli was in a lighthearted mood. His business was booming, and every table was ringed with customers intently watching hotly contested games of eight ball, nine ball, and straight pool. Pocket billiards, pool, was a popular game with the pottery workers at any time, but on Saturdays, the day after payday, the stakes were high. Sometimes there were so many players at one table that the men who drew a high pill number never had a chance to shoot.

Joel Ohlsen liked to drop into Sorelli's on Saturdays, but he was careful to park his car at the Ferrises' house in the next block. His father seldom looked right or left when he was driving to and from the pottery, but Joel didn't care to risk being seen.

The crowd from the pottery didn't like Joel very much. But the workers didn't mind getting a little of J. P.'s money without working for it, even though they did say it was like taking candy from a baby. Fats could make a show of his money here and buy a certain amount of attention even when he lost—which was most of the time.

Mike greeted Joel with a smile and waved toward the back of the room. "They're just starting on table nine, Ohlsen, if you want to play."

It was nearly midnight before Joel lost all the money he had in his pocket, and nearly one o'clock when he tiptoed up the stairs to his room at home. J. P. was always early to bed and early to rise, and Joel knew he'd be grounded if his father heard him coming home that late.

CHAMPIONSHIP BALL

Although Mrs. Ohlsen often pleaded with Joel to come home early, she never told J. P. about their son's late hours. On the few occasions J. P. missed him, Joel had said he was studying at Wheels's. This was always a safe alibi, and J. P. never went to the flats, the industrial area, after dark, except when there was an emergency at the plant.

As Joel stood before his bathroom mirror brushing his teeth, the image reflected in the glass wore a sullen look. Why did he keep on hanging around Sorelli's dump when everyone kept taking him for a ride? Why did everyone pick on him all the time . . . chumps like Chip Hilton? They used to play together from morning to night when they were kids. He had licked Chip in an almost-fair fight, hadn't he?

Something stirred in the boy's memory. After all, he was the one who had built up that quarrel and kept it alive, wasn't he? And the fight—well, he wasn't too proud of his end of it. Still, Chip did have all the luck. That smashed leg? Yes, but didn't the guy have it coming to him anyway?

Why should everybody make a hero of Hilton? Just because his dad had been an All-American, why should Chip throw his weight around? Did people think you were a nobody if you didn't wear a big VF and if you weren't one of Rockwell's pets? Why be a kid all your life? You had to be a man of the world these days.

What right did that bunch like Chip and Biggie and all those losers at the pottery have to look down on an Ohlsen, and why did he always have to lose at pool with all those clowns laughing at him?

Joel Ohlsen turned off the light and climbed into bed feeling very sorry for himself. Someday he'd get even with the whole crowd, but even this realization was of little comfort as he lay there wide awake in the dark.

CHAPTER 4

Three-Man Basketball

THE BIG table was loaded with steaming food, and Mary Hilton was mothering the boys, feigning worry about their appetites. She liked having the boys around and always enjoyed their discussions and was amazed at their teenage appetites. Chip's friends would have been surprised at how well Mary Hilton knew them and cared about their interests and ambitions.

Once or twice a week, usually on Friday evenings and sometimes on Sunday afternoons, Chip would invite some of the guys over for dinner. What a dinner it would be! Mrs. Hilton was a great cook. Today, Chip had invited the three basketball veterans—Speed, Red, and Miguel. Taps Browning and Soapy Smith didn't need invitations—they just barged in—claiming they had standing reservations at the Hilton home.

Talk at the table ranged from exams to term papers to lab books to teachers. After dinner and after dishes—

Taps and Soapy were in charge—the conversation centered on sports.

"How's it feel to be through with football, Speed?" asked Taps.

"Great, no more grass drills!"

"Going out for basketball right away?"

"Sure!" Speed looked at Taps in surprise. "Why not?"

"Thought you might be tired—"

"I never get tired!" Speed was emphatic.

"Well, ya know, a week's rest wouldn't do you any harm," interposed Soapy.

"Yes, and you might get stale," ventured Taps.

"You gotta be good to be stale," flashed Speed.

"Rock says staleness is due to a tired mind," volunteered Red Schwartz.

"That lets Speed out." Soapy grinned. "He doesn't ever have to worry about brain fatigue."

"What brain?" challenged Red.

"Soapy, stop trying to yank my chain." Speed remained cool and calm to the raucous laughter that accompanied the good-natured digs.

Miguel changed the subject. "See the Rock yesterday, Chip?" he asked.

"Sure did!"

"Do any manager's work?"

"No, we looked at the tape of last year's Weston game, and Coach gave me the rundown on my job. Looks tough!"

"You'll soon find out!" Red Schwartz shook his head as he spoke. "Greg had to do everything—set up the tickets, the gate passes, take charge of the ticket money, keep score, help Pop with game-day duties, check equipment, and a thousand other things—to say nothing of putting up with Rock when he went temperamental."

"He gave me an outline," continued Chip. "I think Greg must have cloned four other guys," he added with a long sigh.

"Four other guys is right," agreed Red. "Greg took a lot of punishment from Rock."

"Rock isn't so bad," interrupted Speed. "He might bawl a guy out once in a while, but no one else better do it."

"Yeah," agreed Red, "when Coach is with you, he's with you! He's loyal, but he sure makes you work."

"Speaking of that," said Speed, "remember last year when Rock and Jenkins tangled? 'Member, Chip?"

"I saw that game," Soapy bubbled excitedly. "What was wrong with those guys?"

"It was all because of Greg," said Speed.

"What happened?" asked Taps.

"It's a long story. Chip, you tell it."

"No, you tell it," protested Chip.

"Go ahead, Speed," urged Miguel.

"You really want to hear it? You guys were there!"

"I never did know the inside story," said Soapy.

"Here's the deal: no story—no more dessert," announced Red.

"OK! OK!" laughed Speed. "I'll tell the story."

The boys listened attentively. "Greg was keeping score, as you know," he continued, "and it was a tough game. Delford's high scorer was a guy by the name of Bartlett and he was hot. Nobody could hold him. Coach knew Bartlett was weak on the defense and told Chip to keep cutting and to go under the basket and use an underhand layup when he shot to score, or at worst be fouled.

"Chip shielded the ball with his body so Bartlett couldn't block it—but he did foul him," said Speed.

"Look!" He imitated an underhand shot. "It's a shot that's hard to guard, and if it isn't stopped, it's an easy two points. Chip burned him every time he got the ball. Five minutes after the second half started, Bartlett had four personal fouls."

"Wonder why Coach Jenkins let Bartlett guard Chip?" mused Miguel.

"Chip's the best pivot player in the state."

Chip laughed. "Thanks for the compliment, partner."

"Well, they did switch him to Tim Murphy," continued Speed, "and then it was really bad. Right away, Timmy cut under the basket and scored. Bartlett left him alone a couple more times, and Timmy scored both times. Then Bartlett fouled him again, and that was it; he was out of the game."

"Greg sounded the horn, jumped to his feet, and held up five fingers." Chip was excited by the memory.

Speed laughed and broke in. "The referee waved Bartlett out of the game, and then the entertainment began. Coach Jenkins rushed straight off the bench and began to pound the scorer's table with his fist and yell that Greg was a cheat, that Bartlett had only four fouls, that it was a 'homer,' and that Valley Falls was stealing the game. Boy! Was he hot!"

"But how about the scorebooks?" broke in Soapy. "Don't the home team and visiting team scorebooks have to match?"

"Sure, and they did. It wouldn't have made any difference if they hadn't, though—the home scorebook is the official book."

"What did Jenkins say to that?" asked Taps.

"Well, believe it or not, he accused Greg of marking an extra foul against Bartlett before the officials checked the two books at halftime. The Delford manager was too scared to say anything in opposition to Jenkins.

"That's when Greg got upset. I can still remember—Greg got up and said, 'You can't say that about me,' and then," Speed laughed at the memory, "Coach Jenkins shoved him, and Greg fell right over backward and landed on his butt, and there he was—both feet sticking right up in the air behind the table."

"What did the Rock do?" asked Taps.

"Plenty!" broke in Red. "I had a ringside seat for that one. The officials had to separate them; they haven't spoken since!"

"How about that!" marveled Taps. "How did it all end?"

"Oh, we finished the game if you could call it that," said Speed.

"What happened?"

"Well, after they lost Bartlett, we got a big lead on 'em, and then they really started roughing us up."

"That's Delford every time," someone said.

"The officials were calling fouls left and right," continued Speed, "and pretty soon both teams were down to their last five men. Then, with about ten minutes to go, Delford lost their fifth man on personals and had only four players left. Rock offered to let the fifth man stay in the game, but Jenkins wouldn't have any part of that. He was sore, and you could hear him ranting and raving all over the place. Said he expected that kind of officiating at Valley Falls and that Delford couldn't win if ten men played."

"He's a big crybaby," Rodriguez grunted.

"He's that, all right," nodded Red.

"Rock was too smart for Jenkins though," continued Speed. "He left only four of us in the game, too; four

Valley Falls players against four Delford men! But that was nothing! About two minutes later, Delford lost *another* man and that left them with only three players on the floor. Then Coach took me out, and that's the way the game ended—Chip and Hal Bird and Tim Murphy against three of the Delford men—three against three."

"Who won?" asked Taps.

"We did. The other highlight of the game was that, for the first time I can remember, Rock didn't give us a pep talk between halves. You see, Delford elected to use the locker room right next to ours, and Jenkins hollered and screamed so loudly at his Delford players all through the intermission that Coach just sat down with the rest of us and listened—and then when Jenkins finished he said, 'Well, boys, I can't compete with that act. Let's go!'"

"He didn't give a halftime talk at all?" asked Taps.

"Nope!"

"How bad did ya beat them?"

"Ten, fifteen points—something like that."

"Jenkins sure hates the Rock," said Chip. "Every time we play them, Jenkins gets out of control and puts on a show." He stood up and started out of the room.

"Where do you think you're going?" asked Taps.

"Got to get down to the Sugar Bowl and clean up the place. It's pretty near eleven o'clock."

"Reminds me," said Red. "I've got two lab books past due."

Speed startled them all by crashing the piano keys. "Guess we all better do some studying," he said.

An hour later, Chip's duties at the Sugar Bowl were completed with Browning's help. Taps quietly closed the

Hilton front door and followed Chip through the dimly lit hallway and up the stairs. Chip sat down at his desk and shuffled through some papers. "Here's that English paper I was telling you about," he said.

"All finished?"

"Just about. Tell me what you think."

Taps sat on the bed, reading the paper as his unlaced high-tops plopped to the floor. "Guess I might as well stay all night," he muttered. "Folks are all asleep." Mrs. Browning often joked about whether Taps lived at home or next door at the Hilton home.

He read in silence. After a few minutes he looked up and nodded his head enthusiastically.

"Say, this is good! Where'd you get all the history and stuff?"

"From the books Coach Rockwell loaned me."

"Well, you've sure got a lot of basketball stuff in here I've never even heard about." As he slipped under the covers, he added, "That oughta go in the *Yellow Jacket!*"

"I got a kick out of writing it," said Chip.

Chip clicked off the lights and crawled into the single bed opposite Taps. A little later he heard his mother's footsteps stop in the hall outside the door. She had come to see if he was all right. Even when she went to bed early, Mrs. Hilton never rested easy until Chip was home safe in bed.

CHAPTER 5

Nicknames Win Games

TAPS PACED his steps with Chip's slow gait as the two friends neared the high school. At the foot of the long, stone steps, Biggie Cohen joined them.

"Hi ya, Chipper. Hey, Taps."

On their way up the steps, Taps and Biggie held back so Chip's progress would not be hastened. Steps were not so much of a handicap now. Doc's brace was something! Sometimes he hardly realized it was there.

As they neared the top flight, Joel Ohlsen and Wheels Ferris caught up with them.

"Hah! Check out the sympathy act, Wheels," snickered Fats. "Looks like the athletes can't take it."

Chip completely ignored the digs, but Taps squared his shoulders and took a deep breath. Taps looked seven feet tall as he clenched his fists, stopped, and glared at his large tormentor.

"Come on, Taps, forget him!" Chip grabbed Taps by the arm.

Ohlsen and Ferris reached the top landing, and as he opened the front door, Joel couldn't resist a final dig. "Don't rush, Wheels. School can't possibly start until the number-one used-to-be arrives."

Chip's blood boiled. There was cold loathing in the gray eyes he rose toward Ohlsen. "Someday that big mouth of yours will show up with some teeth missing, Fats."

"You'll never see that day, grandstander. You or any of your alley friends." Joel turned his mocking eyes deliberately toward Biggie and moved through the door.

Biggie made a quick move toward the door and then stopped. His tight lips and squared jaw indicated the effort he was exerting to control himself. Then, drawing a deep breath, he unclenched his hands and shook his head. "Someday I'm gonna—ah, never mind! Let's get to class," he muttered.

That afternoon, Chip hurried down to the locker room. Stopping in the doorway of Pop's training room, he sniffed the air appreciatively. To an athlete, the most wonderful smell in the world is that intangible locker-room aroma that accumulates from the ever-present medicine kits, wintergreen, rubbing alcohol, and analgesics. Back again at practice. This was more like it!

A few minutes later, Chip walked up the stairs to the gym. Coach Rockwell, sitting on the top row of the bleachers, shifted his sharp, black eyes from player to player. The coach looked fit all right. His plain, gray warm-up suit couldn't conceal his muscular build. Chip had never thought much about the Rock's size or his age. He could be pressing sixty, all right, but he didn't look it. His hair was still black, and he still had most of it. He stood above five feet ten, and he could handle his 180 pounds like a cat. He was compact and well-proportioned. When practice was under way, the Rock worked as hard as the players, his eyes darting here and there, never missing a trick.

Chip wondered if he had forgotten anything. "I guess not," he murmured to himself. "Balls all pumped up. Rock's sound system all set, ready to be snapped on. Players' shoes fitted. Practice gear issued."

Valley Falls's new hopefuls, all equipped with white shorts, white jerseys, practice shoes, and socks, were—as Pop would say—rarin' to go.

Chip sat in the bleachers opposite Coach Rockwell, watching the players warm up before practice time. The hands on the big gym clock showed five minutes to four o'clock. Although the coach had been working with the veterans for the past week, this was the first formal practice of the season.

Chip's eyes ranged over the squad. Most of the tryouts were small. In fact, they looked like middle school kids. Valley Falls's team would be small this year, he was thinking. There were only two players taller than six-two, Taps and Bill English, a freshman who was six-three.

The players really felt good—and showed it—cutting up, shouting, slapping, stealing the ball from one another, running aimlessly here and there, and passing and shooting carelessly without pattern or purpose.

Engrossed in watching the guys warm up, Chip missed the minute hand leaping to one minute after four o'clock and was startled when the shrill sound of Coach Rockwell's whistle brought everyone to attention.

NICKNAMES WIN GAMES

"All right, boys, put on your sweat shirts and take seats over there on the bleachers."

Chip thought to himself, *Man! I fell down on the very first real minute of my job. I was supposed to tell Coach Rockwell it was four o'clock.* Was it imagination, or did he really detect a grim glare in his direction from the coach? He moved down to the sound system. At least he'd have that ready if Coach asked for it.

Glancing around with a smile, Rockwell said, "The first thing we've got to do now is get acquainted. Hilton, come here."

"Yes, Coach," replied Chip, as he moved to the coach's side.

"Boys, I guess you all know Hilton by this time. However, we'll start just as if we didn't know him. Get one of those big cards, Chip."

Chip soon returned with a large white card.

"All right, good! Now I want you to mark down on this card the nickname of every player on the squad. We'll start with yours." He spelled out the name. "C-h-i-p, Chip Hilton."

"Yes, sir."

"OK. Now, let's have last year's lettermen," continued the coach. "Morris, I guess everybody knows your nick-name—it's been in print enough. Put down 'Speed' for Morris."

Chip rapidly wrote the names that were called out: Chip, Speed, Mike, and Red. This couldn't be all the bas-ketball lettermen in school, could it? Then he remembered that last year's team had been a veteran outfit. Only he and Speed had been on the starting five, although Red Schwartz and Miguel "Mike" Rodriguez saw lots of play-ing time. Soapy Smith had been a second-stringer.

Chip's thoughts were interrupted by the coach. "In case you new players don't understand what this is all about, I'll explain. Every player's name must be so thoroughly known to the other members of the squad that not a precious second's time will be lost when it's necessary to attract his attention.

"We always start the season by having a name drill," he continued. "The names you give us now will be used all year, and we have to learn them thoroughly. These names will help our teamwork. That right, Miguel?"

"Sure is, Coach!" he nodded his head in agreement.

Rockwell called for the card and read off the names Chip had written: "*Chip* Hilton, *Speed* Morris, *Taps* Browning, *Mike* Rodriguez, *Red* Schwartz, and *Soapy* Smith." Then he went through the list of freshmen: "*Matt* and *Ryan,* the Scott twins, *Sandman* Sanders, *Lefty* Peters, and *Bill* English."

As the coach read the names from the card, Chip again realized the squad's limitations. Most high schools had seventy or eighty boys trying out the first day of practice, and here was one of the leading teams of the state with only a handful of candidates.

"All right," called Rockwell, "now we'll try the name drill. We'll see if we can learn these nicknames right now. Speed, you, Mike, Taps, Red, and Soapy go down under the north basket." He flipped the ball to Speed Morris, and the five players dashed down to the end of the floor and stood waiting.

Turning to the rest of the squad, the coach continued, "Now, one of you choose four others and take the south basket. English, I mean Bill, suppose you take charge."

Motioning toward the portable sound system he said, "This thing all right, Chip?"

NICKNAMES WIN GAMES

"Yes, sir," Chip replied, flipping the power switch and listening anxiously for the familiar hum that signified the system was warming up.

Coach Rockwell took three quick steps up the bleachers, trailing the long cord that connected the microphone to the instrument box. "Heads up, now," he told them. "In this practice the player who has the ball—you take the ball up there, Speed—the man who has the ball dribbles, pivots, turns, or stops, but never passes the ball until he hears his name and recognizes the teammate who calls out. Then he passes the ball to that player. If you freshmen will watch Speed's team, you'll see what I mean. OK, Speed, go ahead!"

Speed dribbled hard for the basket, threw a stop with both feet, and then threw a hard chest pass to Red Schwartz who had screamed, "Speed!" Taps Browning suddenly cut by Red and hollered, "Red!" He received the ball so quickly he fumbled momentarily. Recovering quickly, he sent the ball with a solid bounce pass to Soapy Smith who had yelled, "Hey, Taps!" Soon the air was ringing with "Soapy—Taps—Red—Mike—Speed!"

It was a killer of a practice, and Coach Rockwell knew it. He soon blew his whistle and turned to the freshmen at the other end of the floor.

"All right, Bill, let's go."

This was different. Chip recognized the indecision and lack of confidence immediately. Bill dribbled the ball for ten or fifteen seconds before someone called out— uncertainly. The ball was no longer flying through the air with the zip that had characterized the play of the veterans. Suddenly the coach's whistle shrilled and, after one or two passes, the boys came to a halt.

"That's terrible! What's the trouble, Bill?"

"Well, Coach, I guess we don't know each other very well."

"Yes, and what else?" Rockwell pressed.

"Well, I guess that's the biggest trouble," Bill answered.

"No, it isn't." Coach Rockwell handed the microphone to Chip and leaped down the bleachers. "Let's do a little supposing here. We're playing an important game—a point behind and five seconds to play. There—Speed Morris has the ball. I'm his teammate. I'm under the basket, and there isn't an opponent within twenty feet of me. Five seconds to play, remember! I could score easily if I could only get the ball, but I'm stammering around trying to think of his name, and when I *do* think of it, I call 'Speed.'" The coach's "Speed" was almost a whisper; it couldn't be heard ten feet away. "What's wrong with that, Soapy?"

"Same thing that's wrong with Bill's group, Coach! You ought to yell!" Soapy snapped aggressively.

"All right, you show us. Get up there under the basket and call for the ball. Show these boys how to do it!"

Soapy screamed, "SPEED! SPEED!"

"Louder! Louder!" persisted Rock, and the whole squad laughed as Soapy almost raised the roof screaming "SPEED!" Speed Morris threw the ball the length of the court almost simultaneously, and Soapy reached up and put the ball in the basket.

"That's how nicknames win ball games," said Coach Rockwell in a satisfied voice as he walked back to the bleachers.

CHAPTER 6

Soapy's Dummy Practice

COACH ROCKWELL sat at his desk painstakingly writing a letter. It was not often the coach wrote his own letters. Usually, he tossed his mail to the office secretary and confined his writing to a few scribbled signatures. But this particular letter called for his personal attention, he thought, and when he finished writing, he sat back pensively in his swivel chair, reading the message through from beginning to end:

> Dear Mrs. Hilton,
>
> Thanks for your kind words in the note you sent Mrs. Rockwell and me. Your concerns about Chip are very understandable. However, he has applied himself so enthusiastically to his job as manager of the basketball team that I feel sure you need have no further misgivings concerning his happiness.

CHAMPIONSHIP BALL

During my conversations with Chip, he has expressed disappointment, of course, that his injury prevents his playing, but at no time has he complained. His chief interest, like most boys, is in sports. I know you understand that. It is perfectly natural, and, personally, I feel the more he immerses himself in his schoolwork and basketball, the less he will worry about his leg.

You may be sure I recognize his mental state. His heart and soul were set on playing basketball this year, and he may yet. At any rate, Doc Jones says the leg might be well enough to enable him to play a little baseball next spring. Both Doc and I will watch him carefully.

Chip is a resilient young man. I know he will bounce back—he's made that way.

You may be sure your letter will be held in absolute confidence.

Sincerely,
Henry Rockwell

Coach Rockwell glanced at the office clock. It was 3:30. He slipped the letter in an envelope, sealed it tightly, and placed it thoughtfully in the outgoing mail basket. He glanced around the office and then walked over to the picture of Big Chip Hilton that hung on the wall. Looking up at the picture, he muttered, "He's a good kid, old-timer." Then he turned and entered the coaching staff's dressing room. In a few minutes he reappeared in his gray warm-up suit and hurried off to the gym.

SOAPY'S DUMMY PRACTICE

At the sound of Coach Rockwell's whistle, the boys moved quickly to the bleachers and put on their sweat shirts. That whistle meant business, and they had all learned it was unwise to take one more shot or one more dribble. That was one of Rock's pet peeves, and too bad for the player who didn't stop immediately when he heard the whistle!

Rockwell glanced along the bleachers at the boys who were sitting there looking at him expectantly. "We're really going to grind this afternoon," he began, "but before we start our regular workout, we'll review a bit. First, there's no room for hot shots on this team, and we're not interested in individual acclaim. Just to avoid mistakes, we'll clear up a few things."

He turned to Mike Rodriguez. "Mike, s'pose you explain why we have medicine ball and ball-handling practice every day."

Mike straightened up. "Medicine ball practice is what I call our basketball tuneup drills. We use a medicine ball to develop and strengthen our fingers and muscles. Then when we change to a basketball, it feels as light as a feather, and we're able to control the ball more effectively."

"That's right." The coach signaled to Frank Watts for one of the striped medicine balls.

The medicine ball was the size of a basketball, but many times heavier. As the coach stood there holding it in both hands, he kept flipping and turning it with the tips of his fingers. Suddenly, he threw the heavy ball to Mike Rodriguez. "All right, Mike, Taps, Speed, Soapy, and Red come out here and go through the drill. Don't take off your sweat shirts—only be a second."

The boys leaped to their feet and quickly formed a circle.

"Snap pass!" Coach Rockwell called out. The ball was thrown from one player to another from a position between the chest and the waist with a snap of the fingers.

"Up above!" he ordered. Immediately, the striped ball was passed back and forth as high above their heads as the boys could reach.

On the command, "Downstairs!" the boys spread their feet wide apart and, bending over like football centers, carried the medicine ball far back between the legs. Straightening up quickly, they flipped the ball as hard as they could to a teammate.

"OK, that's enough," Rockwell cried, and the five players trotted back to the bleachers.

"What's meant by slow-motion, Taps?" he asked, looking at the big center whose legs extended over three rows of bleachers. Taps struggled to his feet. "That's movie lingo, Coach. Slow like a movie—to develop form."

"All right, show us a shot from the pivot position— slow-motion."

Chip flipped a ball to Taps as he reached the floor and the big athlete dribbled quickly beneath the basket where he gave his impression of a slow-motion shot.

"Notice Taps has that ball right on his fingertips," broke in the coach just as Taps faked and perfectly executed the shot he and Chip had been practicing so consistently. The ball kissed off the backboard and dropped cleanly through the basket.

"Good! That was excellent, Taps," Rockwell said, pleased.

It was easy to understand why Coach Rockwell was concentrating on Taps. The success of the season undoubtedly depended on how well Taps could handle his height under both the defensive and offensive boards.

SOAPY'S DUMMY PRACTICE

Taps would have to play against one and sometimes two big opponents—athletes taller and heavier. He was still all arms and legs. He had a strong frame, large hands and shoulders, but he hadn't filled out yet.

Taps dribbled back to the bleachers and snapped the ball to Chip with a grin. The look the two exchanged almost seemed to say, "Man, that old practice is beginning to pay off!"

Coach Rockwell next singled out Soapy Smith. "What's a simulation practice, Soapy?" he asked. "That's right, you call it 'dummy' practice, don't you, Soapy?"

A few chuckles could be heard as Soapy laboriously rose to his feet. "Well, dummy practice, Coach, is playing make-believe."

Everyone grinned as Soapy grew serious and continued belligerently, "I know we always use it when you come back from scouting. Sometimes we dummy practice two, three days."

Soapy sat down again with a sigh of relief. He was glad *that* was over!

"That's good—far as it goes," confirmed Rock, "but you'll have to do better than that. What else?"

Soapy struggled to his feet again and began uncertainly. "Well, all I know is when you scout a team, you always dress up the reserves. Soapy stopped and looked around with a grin. "That's guys like me." Everyone laughed as he continued, "Then we get numbers like the players we're imitatin'—if he's a dribbler one of us is s'posed to dribble like he does—and if he's a scorer, one of us mirrors his shot."

Soapy was really going strong now and getting into the subject. "Then you tell us what kind of offense and defense the other team uses," Soapy said, grinning again, "and we dummies practice and play just like the other team does!"

Chet Stewart, standing at the board the coaches always used for scribbling the plays on, snorted, shook his head, and whispered audibly, "Dummies is right!"

"Is that all there is to it?" prodded Coach Rockwell.

"No, sir—no, sir!" Soapy was positive. "After we've got it down, we play against the first string and use slow-motion and dummy practice to get ready to beat 'em."

Rockwell smiled. "Thanks, Soapy. Now," he continued, "before we go through our repertoire of passes, I want to give out these photocopied sheets of the give-and-go plays." He handed the sheets of paper to Chip, and soon every boy was scanning the paper carefully.

"We'll practice these plays every night until we master them, but before we do that, I want you to study the outlines carefully. Morris and Schwartz are experts with this backcourt maneuver, and they'll help you newcomers with the plays if you'll just ask them. I've erased the three-point line—plenty of lines in the diagram now to keep you busy," Rockwell laughed. "I think the outlines are clear enough, but if they're not, drop in my office any time, and I'll be glad to go over them with you.

SOAPY'S DUMMY PRACTICE

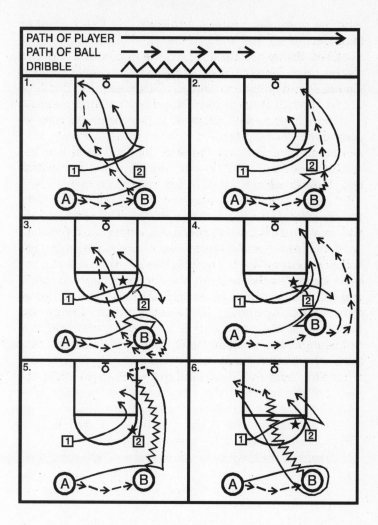

PATH OF PLAYER
PATH OF BALL
DRIBBLE

1.

2.

3.

4.

5.

6.

The plays were familiar to Chip. He knew them by heart although his work under the basket had never required him to use them. The plays Rockwell had placed on the sheet were but a few of the many give-and-go plays Speed and Red had mastered. Coincidentally, Rockwell called for the two backcourt experts just at that moment.

"Speed, you and Red show us the passes we use—in slow-motion."

Speed and Red hit the floor as soon as the words were out of Rockwell's mouth, and Chip had to hurry to get the ball to them.

"Let's have the baseball pass, first," Rockwell cried.

Speed carried the ball to a position beside his right ear and assumed much the same stance as a baseball catcher takes when throwing to second base. His elbow extended even with his shoulder; with exaggerated slowness, he brought the forearm forward, turning his shoulder and extending his arm as he followed through by extending his spread fingers along the flight of the ball.

Red caught the ball deftly and repeated the same pass with his left hand.

"Why do we extend the spread fingers along the flight of the ball and then down toward the floor after we've thrown the ball, Mike?" asked the coach.

"That gives it speed," he explained. "That last little flip puts spin on the ball—gives it a lot of zip."

"Yes, but we have to be careful about this spin, don't we?" The coach looked at Mike questioningly.

"Yes, sir," Rodriguez replied.

"But why?"

"We have to be careful about using spin. Baseball passes are used for long throws, and if we put left-to-right or right-to-left spin on the ball, it will curve and maybe cause a turnover," said Mike.

"That answer is absolutely right! Speed, go down under the south basket. Red, you throw the ball and be careful of that spin."

Speed reached the basket almost before the coach finished speaking, and Red threw the ball like a base-ball—true and straight—to Speed's waiting hands.

"Roll it back."

Speed used the form and follow through of a bowler as he sent the ball spinning back to Red. As Red bent over to retrieve the ball, Coach Rockwell continued, "Now, Red, throw the ball to Speed with the wrong kind of spin."

Red again cocked his arm like a baseball catcher, but this time, at the last moment of release, he turned his fingers and wrist clockwise toward the right. The spinning ball started straight enough, but before it reached him, Speed was forced to take two or three quick steps away from the basket in order to catch the wildly careening ball.

"Well, I guess that demonstration makes it clear enough why you have to use reverse spin on a long pass. That curving ball drew Speed away from the basket and, in a game, might have cost us two points."

Chip observed nodding heads all along the line.

Soon the whole squad was out on the floor, and Rock was calling for the passes and drills he wanted. After thirty minutes of action work, the schedule called for shooting practice. This was the part the guys liked best. Everyone likes to shoot!

After a short, slow-motion rehearsal, the coach called for running layup shots. The squad was happy and cheered every successful shot.

CHAMPIONSHIP BALL

Without thinking, Chip moved out on the court behind the basket and began throwing the loose balls back to the players.

The angry shrill of the whistle brought everything and everyone to a sudden halt. Chip stood holding a ball as Coach Rockwell came clattering down from the "roost" high in the bleachers and strode directly toward him.

"What do you think you're doing?" he demanded.

"Why, just throwin' the balls back, Coach," Chip said hesitantly.

"You know my rule about this floor, don't you?"

"Why, sure, Coach, but—"

"No buts! No one's permitted on this floor with street shoes. You get into that equipment room and get a pair of basketball shoes and you wear 'em out here every day from now on. I want to see you shootin' a few baskets too!" A slow smile spread over his lips. "You don't have to shoot baskets with your leg, do you?"

Chip smiled happily. "No, *sir!*"

CHAPTER 7

Forty-Four on Reserve

VALLEY FALLS'S basketball hopefuls had looked forward to this particular Saturday morning with eagerness because the town's sportswriters and photographers were expected. The dressing room was filled with commotion when Chip arrived. Chet Stewart greeted him with a smiling, "Good afternoon, Mr. Hilton." Chip quickly caught the sarcasm in Stewart's words and immediately pitched in to help out. Chet and Pop were working feverishly to fit each boy with the proper size uniform and warm-up suit. The assistant managers, Frank Watts and Herb Holden, were hustling to and from the equipment room carrying all kinds of jerseys, shoes, socks, and warm-up suits.

The Valley Falls colors, scarlet and white, combined to create an impressive and flashy warm-up suit. Every varsity candidate desperately wanted to earn one. In fact, the colors accentuated the size of even the smallest

CHAMPIONSHIP BALL

guys. This was a bit of Coach Rockwell's psychology. He made his players look big, one way or another.

The photographers had already set up their cameras out on the court and were talking to Coach Rockwell. When all the boys had finished dressing, he moved down to the south end of the court and joined in passing the ball.

This was no ordinary practice session; it was one of the last steps in selecting the team. Once a player was issued a playing uniform and warm-up with a big number adorning its front and back, it was difficult to separate that number from his playing identity. Chet had discussed this topic with Pop and Chip many times, stressing the importance of a number in a boy's basketball career. Most players stuck to one number throughout their playing days. Speed Morris, for instance, had worn number 24 ever since he was a freshman.

Rockwell also believed in team unity. The only name on the uniforms was Valley Falls. Rockwell often said, "We're a team! The name on the front—Valley Falls—is what's important. When you play in the NBA, then you can wear your name on the back!"

Looking at the brightly dressed players, Chip felt a deep ache in his heart for the first time in weeks. If things had been different, he'd be wearing a big 44. Well, as Rock had said, maybe he wasn't through yet. Anyway, Chet had said Rock wasn't going to give out number 44. That helped a lot. Maybe he'd be wearing that number again . . . maybe before the season was over.

When Doc had removed the cast from Chip's leg, he had said the surgery on the ankle was a success, even though the injured leg was stiff and atrophied. Time would tell.

Chip had gone through a few minor adjustments, and the brace was firm on his leg. He felt like a million bucks today—he was, as Pop always said, rarin' to go!

The big clock showed 3:45 P.M. as Chip came out of the dressing room. Coach Rockwell and the photographers were talking near the hall. Taps Browning was standing under one of the side baskets, and Chip joined his friend.

"Say, Chip," Taps began seriously, "you know that hook shot you showed me before you got hurt?"

"You mean with a step-away?"

"Yes," answered Taps. "Wish you'd help me with it. I could get a lot of points with that shot." He handed the ball to Chip and waited.

"If my—" Chip caught himself just in time. "It's a good shot, Taps," he said, "and your height makes it hard to stop." He juggled the ball in his hands a couple of times and then turned his back to the basket.

"Look!" Chip half-turned his head, shoulders, and hips to the right and faked a shot with his left hand. Almost without a pause, he then whirled to the left, took a step away from the basket, and following a short leap in the air, transferred the ball to his right hand, dropping it cleanly through the hoop.

"Smooth," breathed Taps, "if I could only do that."

Chip had surprised himself. He had pushed off with his injured leg and landed on the floor without the slightest twinge of pain. He recovered the ball and breathed a sigh of relief. "You'll do it, or I'll know why. Try it in slow-motion, Taps."

For the next fifteen minutes they worked on Chip's favorite shots. Taps was coming along fast. "Dunk one, Taps," Chip encouraged. Taps moved back to the free-throw line and then dribbled hard for the basket. Leaping high in the air, he snapped the ball down through the basket without touching the rim.

"Hey! Do that again," called a photographer.

Taps grinned at Chip, walked back to the free-throw circle, dribbled hard for the basket, and, leaping high in the air, repeated the performance. Taps dunked the ball a half-dozen times, and the photographers got several shots of the action. Afterward, each player posed individually with the ball.

When the individual pictures had been taken, Coach Rockwell called all the boys together for a squad picture. Chip had moved up on the bleachers, and his heart jumped when Coach Rockwell called to him, "Come here, Chip. You're part of this team—get in the picture. Stand over here by me."

"How about Chet and Pop?" Chip asked.

"That's right. Tell 'em to come over."

After the photographers had finished with the players, they asked Coach Rockwell for several individual poses. Chet, Pop, and the boys then really had a chance to see Rock squirm. First, the visitors asked for a picture with a ball, then one underneath the row of Valley Falls banners, and finally one of the coach sitting at a table— supposedly writing the names of this year's starting five.

"Chip," called Coach Rockwell when the photographers had completed their work, "go in the gym office and get a couple of rosters and schedules for Mr. Kennedy and Mr. Williams."

Joe Kennedy was sports editor of the *Times,* and Pete Williams was the basketball expert of the *Post.*

"All right, let's go," called Chet Stewart. "Get those suits off and hand them in to Pop. We've still got work to do."

FORTY-FOUR ON RESERVE

Later, Coach Rockwell, Williams, and Kennedy stood near the gym office and watched the practice.

"Isn't that Hilton out there, Rock?" asked Williams, motioning toward Chip, who was shooting baskets with Taps Browning.

"Yes, that's him! Bad leg just about broke his heart."

"How is that leg anyway?" inquired Kennedy.

"Takes a long time for an ankle fracture to heal," Rockwell said regretfully. "Sometimes they're never any good for athletics again, you know, and sometimes they turn out stronger than ever."

"He had terrific possibilities," said Kennedy. "He would have been a sure bet for a scholarship anywhere—he and Morris."

"Sure," Coach Rockwell agreed. "State's been after the pair of them since they were freshmen."

"Guess you haven't forgotten Big Chip, have you, Rock?" smiled Williams.

"No—I never will, I guess! He was the greatest athlete I ever coached! Coaches hope and pray for an athlete like him—just once in a coaching career! I've been blessed twice. Chip can do more things, and don't forget he's a couple of years younger than his dad was when he played in high school."

"That's right!" nodded Kennedy.

"Hilton handles himself better than I expected," observed Williams.

"Yes, but he can't do much with that brace. Doc Jones told me the ankle is really stiff. That's why we're trying to encourage him to work out and loosen it up—we hope!" Coach Rockwell was watching Chip carefully.

"Have to give the kid credit for trying. Well, good luck, Rock," said Kennedy.

"He'll need it!" Williams ominously remarked as the two men turned to leave. "So long, Rock."

After Kennedy and Williams had gone, Rockwell called the players to the middle of the court. "Boys," he said, "you don't have to practice any longer today unless you want to. Suit yourselves. However, the gym will be open for any 'gym-rats' until you've had enough for one day. Right, Pop?"

One by one, the boys dropped out. This was Saturday, and almost every player welcomed the chance to rest. Eventually only Taps and Chip remained.

"I'm sure glad they got the picture of you dunking the ball, Taps."

"Seems to me it's a whole lot like showing off."

"I wouldn't look at it that way. Everybody wants to dunk, but not everybody can actually do it! Just don't do it during the game warm-up or it's a technical."

After a good hour's work, they hit the showers and left the gym, Taps heading for home and Chip toward the Sugar Bowl.

CHAPTER 8

The Young Journalist

CHIP NEEDED help. His thoughts turned to Coach Rockwell, and he decided to pay him a visit. He took the long flight of steps slowly and found the coach seated at his desk with his face buried in a paper. Chip paused at the open door until Rockwell looked up. "Could I see you a minute, Coach?" he asked

"Sure, Chip. Come in, sit down."

"I'll only be a minute, Coach. I—I'd like to get some advice."

"I've got lots of time. I'm just proofreading this week's *Yellow Jacket*." Tapping the pages he held in his hand with a pencil, Rock smiled. "See you're getting into print."

"You mean the basketball article?"

"Yes, Chip, and it's all right too. Dr. Zimmerman makes me proofread the sports page, you know."

"I can wait until you're finished, Coach."

"No need; I'm through. This is a fine article, Chip. It's good reading. Not many kids—athletes either, for that matter—know much about the history of basketball."

"I'm glad you like it, Coach. Harry Nichols did most of the work though."

"Well, anyway, it's good. Now, what's on your mind?"

"That article is actually what I want to talk to you about, Coach. I wrote it originally as a paper for English, but Taps read it and showed it to Harry Nichols. Nichols asked me to let him print it, and I did. Then I got foolish and agreed to write some more stuff. Now I'm in a predicament because I don't know what to write about."

"This story is good, Chip. Of course, I'm a little partial, but why don't you write more about basketball?"

"I'd like to, but I've run out of ideas."

"That's easy," said Coach Rockwell. "If you really want to write basketball, go over to the public library. You'll find all the official basketball guides there, from January 1894, running right up to this year. You'll find records and oddities and all kinds of story material in those little books. They've got all the materials you'll need, all the good stuff. Look for several sources, and you'll find more than enough information."

"That sounds like a super idea, Coach."

"By the way," Rockwell added reflectively, "that library won an argument for me several years ago. The high school coaches held their annual meeting here at Valley Falls High a few years ago, and several of us got to arguing about the zone. You know, Chip, some coaches feel the zone is the only true defense in basketball. Others believe the original philosophy of the game planned defense to be man-to-man."

"I never thought of that."

"The argument started over the first defense. I said that man-to-man was the defense Dr. Naismith intended when he originated the game. Some coaches sided with me, and others said the zone. What an argument we all had!"

"Who was right?"

"You judge. We went to the library and got the first basketball rule book: January 1894. I can still remember the wording: 'When a player is on the defense he should stick to his man like glue, follow him everywhere, try to prevent him from receiving the ball and, if he should receive it, try to keep him from trying for the goal or passing to a teammate.'"

"Then man-to-man was right!"

"Yes," said Coach Rockwell, nodding his head, "and it's the proper defense to start a player out with today, no matter whether he is going to play on a zone team or not. Today's players are faster and quicker, but they know less about how the game is played and its history."

"I'll take your word for it, Coach," laughed Chip.

"Since you're thinking about writing sports, Chip, the best thing you can do is to master the philosophy and history of the games you write about. Your problem right now is to get a good basketball background. You'll have to work that out yourself."

"Do you mind if I'm a little late for practice, Coach? After school's about the only chance I have to get to the library."

"Of course not, Chip. You let practice go for this afternoon. I'll tell Chet I excused you."

"But I—"

"Never mind. School comes first and basketball second. You go to that library."

CHAMPIONSHIP BALL

Right after school, Chip headed off for the Valley Falls Public Library. He climbed the long flight of stone steps without stopping and slowly made his way into the impressive building.

The librarian at the information desk directed him upstairs. Oh, no, more steps! As he approached the reference room, he saw a woman standing behind the half-door.

"May I help you?" she smiled pleasantly.

"Why—why—yes, thanks," faltered Chip, presenting the card the librarian at the information desk had given him. "I'd like to see the basketball guides if I may."

"Certainly. Just a moment." Opening the door, she led him to a table. "You can sit here, and I'll bring the volume you want," she said. "What year do you need?"

"I'd like to have the first ones," said Chip.

"I can bring you only one at a time. They're very valuable, you know."

"They must be!" Chip looked around at the barred windows and grilled door.

"Don't be silly," she said with a smile. "The guides are rare originals, almost priceless! Just wait a minute and I'll bring you the first basketball book."

In a few minutes, she returned and Chip gazed down at a thin little volume: *Basketball Guide* by James A. Naismith—January 1894. Its leaves were yellow and flaky with age. He buried himself in the old tattered volume.

Chip took a good kidding at the Sugar Bowl Thursday evening. As Speed dropped him in front of the store, Chip was greeted by a chorus: "Hey, everybody, look who's here!"

"Well, well, Mr. *Yellow Jacket* is here and in person."

"Hey, it's the Valley Falls sports expert."

THE YOUNG JOURNALIST

Behind the fountain Petey Jackson was reading parts of an article to Ted Williams, Harry Nichols, Red Schwartz, and Biggie Cohen. "Here's our resident author himself," he announced, catching sight of Chip.

"Don't let him give you a hard time, Chip," Ted laughed. "It's darned good!" He waved Chip to a stool beside him in front of the fountain and handed him a copy of the *Yellow Jacket*. "Did you see it?" he asked.

"Yes, I did, Ted. You think it's OK?"

"Mr. Hilton," Harry Nichols interrupted with mock seriousness, "my paper, the *Yellow Jacket,* has authorized me to offer you a weekly contract of five thousand dollars for the exclusive use of your material. Naturally, we expect to feature your stories in our national syndicate."

Chip laughed. "That's not enough—but let's do lunch sometime."

"Aw, take the five thousand," advised Red Schwartz.

"I'll take it up with my agent," began Chip.

"Well, Harry, show him the money!" Biggie laughed.

Nichols laughed and then added seriously, "No kidding, Chip, it's the best sports article we've printed this year."

Chip went to the storeroom, and Speed, Biggie Cohen, and Red Schwartz followed.

The subject of basketball and its history, featured in Chip's *Yellow Jacket* article, was continued.

"Dr. Naismith invented the game at Springfield College, didn't he?" asked Red.

"Well, it wasn't exactly called Springfield College then," said Chip. "Dr. Naismith was teaching at the International Y.M.C.A. Training School, which was located in Springfield, Massachusetts, when he invented the game. It's called Springfield College now though."

"Hey, isn't the Basketball Hall of Fame located in Springfield?" asked Red.

"Sure it is. It'd be great to go there sometime and see all the displays. Maybe the summer we graduate," offered Chip.

"Is it true," asked Biggie, "that in the beginning the game didn't have a name?"

"That's right," agreed Chip.

"How come?" asked Biggie.

"Naismith and one of his students, a guy named Mahon, were talking about possible names, and Mahon asked, 'Why not call it Naismith ball?'"

"Why didn't they?"

"Well, Dr. Naismith figured nobody would play a game with a name like that—"

"Probably right," said Red.

"It was simple enough though," Chip continued. "Mahon hit the nail right on the head when he said, 'We've got a basket and a ball; why not call it basketball?'"

"Wait until your mom reads the *Yellow Jacket* and finds out how important Mrs. Naismith was in basketball," said Biggie. "She'll be saying Mrs. Naismith helped Dr. Naismith write the rules."

"Mrs. Naismith was important!" Chip laughed. "Anyway, she was captain of the first girls' basketball team and one of the first spectators ever to see a game."

"Wonder how she met Naismith?" mused Biggie.

"Naismith rented a room in her family's home," said Chip.

"She probably had a crush on him even before the game was invented!" Red chimed in with a laugh.

"She must have been ahead of her time," said Biggie. "In those days women didn't go in for sports much. Think of it, guys! She was playing basketball way back in 1891! History is fun."

CHAPTER 9

Words from the Heart

THE DAYS seemed to fly. The Christmas holidays came and went. Chip couldn't find time for half the things he wanted to do. He was so wrapped up in his schoolwork, sportswriting, and basketball, he hardly had time to think.

Today he was late and tried to take the gym steps two at a time, but the brace restrained him, and he was forced to follow his usual pattern. One, two, three, four . . . twenty-six. Funny, he thought, pausing at his favorite spot on the broad landing and gazing around, his leg hadn't bothered him at all going up those long steps.

Continuing into the building, he hurried through the big trophy foyer and down the long corridor. Offices lined the hall on each side—Coach Rockwell's, Burrell Rogers's, the physical education instructors' lounge, several other VF coaches' offices, and the conference room.

Chip called the hallway "Coaches Alley." An athlete could always find excitement here.

As he approached the conference room, he heard laughter from the squad that had assembled for a strategy session. There was a lull in the clamor as he opened the door, but as soon as he was recognized, he was met by a barrage of greetings:

"You're late, man."

"Hi ya, Chipper."

"Come on in quick—this is good!"

"Hey, guys!" Chip tallied, glancing around the big table. He counted figures as he moved to a chair beside Taps. Yes, they were all there. The guys had relaxed again, and he joined the other players listening to Red Schwartz.

"Yeah, Rock has been giving that pep talk for twenty years," continued Red. He glanced cautiously at the door. Everyone was in a great mood and getting a big kick out of Red. Speed sat beside Red at the head of the big conference table with his back to the door.

"Sure," Red went on, "why, we can always tell when Rock has a banquet coming up. All week he practices his speech on us."

"And are they lousy! They're pretty lame," chimed in Speed.

"Lame is right," grimaced Red.

No one laughed, and in the room's sudden silence Red and Speed, following the direction of everyone else's glance, turned their heads to see Coach Rockwell standing at the door he had quietly opened.

"Oh, man!" moaned Red turning as crimson as the school colors. Gazing at Speed as if looking for help, he managed another, "Oh, man!" before burying his face in his arms folded on the table. Speed was straight-faced and looked perfectly innocent.

Coach Rockwell smiled and said nothing but raised an eyebrow in Red's direction. Walking to the head of the table, Rock's glance shifted rapidly from face to face as he greeted the squad with his usual, "All right, boys, let's go!"

"All present and accounted for, Coach," Chip reported.

"And everybody on time but me," quipped the coach.

"Boys," he went on, "this afternoon I've really got time to say some of the things I should have brought to your attention the first day of practice.

"Teamwork and morale are important factors in all areas of athletics. All the things I'm going to talk about today center on those important factors. Morale means team spirit; it means enthusiastic practices and fighting for the team and the school whether you're on the bench or on the floor.

"Courage is an important attribute in life and in athletics. It takes courage to study when you're tired just as much as it does to fight out there on the court when the going gets tough. Often a game becomes more important to a player than school—that's bad. School's first. Basketball's second. Furthermore, the disaster that ineligibility can bring to a team can't be overemphasized. Certainly it's much better to have a less-able player and be able to use him for the entire season than to have a superstar half a year and then, because of ineligibility, lose him after he's become important to the team.

"All of you are capable of passing your subjects. Half the battle in school is being regular in attendance and keeping up with your homework assignments—"

"We sure get enough homework," muttered Red, trying to redeem himself with Rock.

"Most of you know how I feel about spreading yourself too thin, taking on more activities than you can handle. Sooner or later, something has got to give. You'll wear yourself down so you can't perform in the classroom or on the court. Your grades will suffer, and then the team will suffer. Playing on outside teams interferes with your school and team responsibilities and can cause injuries."

Coach Rockwell's jaw squared as he bit off his words. "You can't go to those practices and play outside ball and also play for Valley Falls High. You'll have to devote your playing to Valley Falls High School exclusively, or you'll have to turn in your uniform! Is that clear?

"So much for playing outside ball. Let's skip strategy for the moment. Plays aren't everything. A successful team must have something more than strategy. First, a successful team possesses a fierce desire to win; second, the will to persevere in practice; and third, team spirit and teamwork—confidence in one another.

"Chip, do you remember the play that won the section championship for us two years ago in the final game against Parkton?"

"I sure do, Coach!"

"Well," prompted Rockwell, "go ahead! Tell us what happened!"

"There were only five minutes to go, and we were six points behind, and Tim Murphy took a time-out. You sent word for us to feed Sy Barrett—and we did! Sy was hot! He hit three quick shots while Parkton was scoring only one point, and then with just a few seconds to go, Sy took a jumper from his favorite spot near the left sideline. We were one point behind with ten seconds to go when he took the shot—but he missed!"

Chip nodded his head toward Speed. "Speed drove in for the rebound and got the ball. He really could have tried a tip-in, but he didn't! He surprised everybody when he hooked the ball right back out to Sy.

"Parkton's players had all rushed back under the basket to get the rebound, and there wasn't anyone near Sy. He took aim, just as though he were practicing, and let the ball fly. Right after he shot, the buzzer sounded, but the ball was in the air and swished through the basket just as though it had eyes—and we won by a point!"

"That was s-o-m-e shot!" marveled Speed, shaking his head at the memory. "You know, Coach, I didn't have the least doubt Sy would bury it."

"Me either!" confirmed Chip. "Old Sy might miss one—but he'd never miss two from the same spot."

Coach Rockwell nodded his head reflectively. "You're right," he agreed. "What I'm trying to bring out here is the fact that Speed and Chip, and the rest of the team, had enough confidence in Barrett to place the responsibility of winning that game solely on Sy's shoulders."

"Don't see how he could be a better shot than Mike," ventured Taps.

"Cut it out!" complained Mike, self-consciously. "Sy was the best shooter who ever played for Valley Falls!"

"Well, I never saw him play," said Taps, "but I'd bet on you!"

"That brings us to practice," broke in the coach.

Everyone leaned a little closer. "Practice is vital! Correct repetition is the secret of basketball success! Lots of high school stars reach the top too soon and feel they don't need to practice. Newspaper headlines often result in enlargement of the occipital bones—commonly known as a swelled head—and when that happens to a player, he has reached his limit. I prefer average basket-ball players who can improve. We have no time here for players with oversized egos, for we all realize we have weaknesses that practice alone can remedy."

Chip had been so engrossed in the meeting that he'd forgotten the time. Now he glanced at his wristwatch—4:35. He caught Coach Rockwell's attention and tapped his watch a few times.

"All right," nodded the coach, "time is short, but before we break up, I'd like to refer to the rules. Valley Falls plays according to the book and uses no fancy blocks or tricks. I've no time for players who resort to arm-pulling, pushing, and holding of uniforms. We play clean basketball! Furthermore, there's only one man on the floor who can talk to the officials—that's the captain! Any player who speaks disrespectfully to the referee comes out of the game—immediately—win or lose. That brings up another important matter, the captain. We'll elect him in the dressing room just before the alumni game!"

CHAPTER 10

Repetition Pays

CHIP HILTON quietly rose from his seat and tiptoed to Dr. "Maggots" Magnus's desk and dropped his history exam booklet on top of the rest. It was his last semester exam, and he had the feeling he'd aced it!

Outside, the cool, crisp air made his blood jump. He was anxious to get to the gym. Maybe Chet or Pop would shoot baskets with him. Coach Rockwell had been driving the team hard—moving, demonstrating, explaining, and forcing the players to rehearse a play or a game situation again and again. Chip thought of Coach Rockwell's pet phrase: "Correct repetition is the secret of basketball success!" Well, this team ought to beat everyone. The players repeated everything they did about fifty times!

He changed quickly and headed up the stairs. Soon the gym was full of players working on individual skills. Chip moved over to a practice basket and sat down on the floor with his feet just touching the free-throw line. From this awkward position, he used only his arms, wrists, and fingers to speed the ball with almost effortless ease into the basket. His accuracy was amazing, and several of the freshman players gathered around and watched him with admiration. Taps trotted over under the basket. Chip shot, and Taps, standing directly under the ring, stretched his long arms above his head and caught the ball just as it dropped through the net.

Speed dashed over, dribbling a ball. "Move over, deadeye!" he called as he dropped down on the court beside Chip. "How about a little competition for an ice cream at the Sugar Bowl?" he challenged.

"OK, you're on," Chip grinned. "Taps, you keep count. Best out of ten."

Red Schwartz dribbled around under the basket and back to Chip's other side. "Can I get in it on this too?"

"Mmm, I can taste that butter pecan already," drawled Speed, poking Chip with his elbow.

"All right, who's first?" interrupted Taps.

"Aw, let the big shot shoot first," someone said.

"You mean me, I presume?" Red quipped, bowing politely.

"Right the first time!" was the comeback.

Red missed the first three shots amid loud and rowdy jeers and jibes, but he finally hit a streak and ended up with five out of ten.

"True to form," snorted Mike. "Fifty-fifty. That's good old Red."

"Good enough to beat you!" retorted Red.

Speed was next and managed to cage seven of his ten shots. All eyes were on Chip now. He missed the first shot and then ripped the cords for nine straight.

REPETITION PAYS

"Nice going, Chip," Taps called, snapping the ball back to him enthusiastically. "Go on, see how long you keep it going!"

Chip continued and, after a shaky tenth and eleventh shot, ran his string to sixteen straight before missing.

Chet Stewart joined the group. "Nice shooting, Chip," he said. "Too bad some of the All-Americans aren't shooting like that!" He glanced at Speed, Red, Taps, and Mike. Then, shaking his head mournfully, he walked away.

Chip limped over to the bleachers and sat down by Frank Watts. Glancing back at the group, he saw Speed, Taps, Red, and Mike standing shoulder to shoulder on the fifteen-foot free-throw line, taking turns shooting fouls while Soapy retrieved the ball. From their determined faces and serious manner, Chip knew Chet's pointed remark had struck home.

"Wish they could all shoot fouls like Mike," Frank said earnestly. "If they could, Valley Falls wouldn't lose many games this year. Coach says about 90 percent of all games between good teams are won on free throws."

"He's sure right," affirmed Chip, nodding his head in agreement. "Mike hit forty-two straight the other afternoon; of course, that was just practice."

Glancing at the big clock on the gymnasium wall, Chip saw there were still ten minutes before regular practice began. What a difference a few weeks can make, he thought. The workouts had been tough, and Coach had lived up to his reputation as a taskmaster, but the guys had loved every minute of it—even when they were griping. Coach sure knew the secret of coaching: "Keep them busy, make it short, and have fun!"

Four of the starting five players were set. Speed was at left forward and sure to be elected captain before the first game. Taps was improving every day. Chip felt a sense of satisfaction in that. He had worked with Taps every afternoon, sometimes for a solid hour. It was funny, Chip reflected, how well he was getting around on his bad leg.

Red Schwartz and Miguel "Mike" Rodriguez were sure of the guard positions. Good old Red—the team's easygoing sparkplug and a great backcourt player, with plenty of drive. And last but not least, Mike, the best shot on the squad. Mike could bury the ball from any place on the court. When Mike concentrated on a shot and got squared up to the basket, just rack up another score!

The fifth spot was wide open, but Chip had already tabbed little Pat "Sandman" Sanders as his choice. Pat and Lefty Peters were fighting with all their might to earn the last starting spot. It didn't matter much who won out; both were good!

Wow! The first game is less than two weeks away . . . seems like only yesterday we were holding the first day of practice.

Frank Watts tapped his shoulder. "Time, Chip," he said, nodding his head in the direction of the clock.

Chip turned and glanced up at the Rockwell's roost, but the coach had already started down from his perch and waved his hand to show he knew the time. The sharp blast of his whistle halted all activity on the court, and the players trotted over to the bleachers.

Rockwell pulled the portable board in front of the seated athletes and got busy with markers and eraser.

"Boys," he captured their attention, "in another ten days we'll be on our way. There's a lot more to basketball than offense and defense. Psychology and strategy are favorite weapons of champions. I'd like to give you one of the valuable weapons a lot of teams use effectively—the press."

He turned back to the whiteboard and expertly drew a number of diagrams and lines on the shiny surface.

Rockwell was expert in using a marker and board or pencil and paper to illustrate what the players were to absorb, practice, and then perform. The replica of a court that he drew on the board was almost perfect.

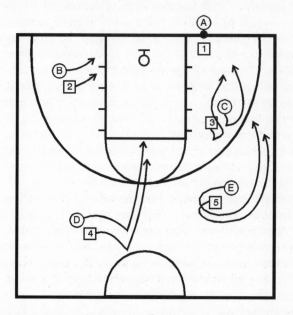

"The defensive players, in this case the squares—1, 2, 3, 4, and 5—have just scored, and their opponents have taken the ball out of bounds under the basket. Instead of retreating beyond the ten-second line and waiting for the team that has just been scored upon to advance the ball across the ten-second line, the scoring players have pressed close to their men and are guarding them all over the court.

"This *team* strategy places the burden of advancing the ball across the ten-second line on the team that has just been scored upon. A bad pass or using more than ten seconds in bringing the ball across the division line or midcourt line will result in possession of the ball by the forcing players—1, 2, 3, 4, and 5. Good, hard defense is rewarded!

"In the closing minutes of a game, when a team is behind in the score, this strategy is imperative. Executing the press effectively may result in a possession or an intercepted pass—and an easy score. The press can also be used to change the tempo of the opposition earlier in the game."

Rockwell paused and searched the eyes of the intense group of boys. He evidently must have seen something in their expressions that pleased him, for he smiled broadly and his voice rang with satisfaction as he continued.

"However, pressing demands the utmost in team play. Each player must concentrate on his immediate opponent and stick with him—no matter where he goes! The emphasis here is on playing each opponent closely and forcing an error. It pays off well, when well-played.

"Think it over, boys. We'll probably have to use the press many times before this season is over. Next week, we'll work it out in practice. Today we'll stick to our fundamentals."

Two hours later, the tired squad welcomed Rockwell's "Hit the showers!" But long after the noisy crowd had left the gym, Taps and Chip still continued to work on their shots and their under-the-basket drills. If repetition was the price, Chip and Taps were sure willing to pay!

First Blood

THE LONG-AWAITED Wednesday of the season's first real scrimmage arrived at last. The big red-and-white scoreboard was all set. It had been readied for the first time since practice had started five weeks ago. Pop pressed buttons and checked the corresponding lights on the board.

Down at the south basket, tall, agile players dashed around and practiced all kinds of shots. Two of these players were members of the Flying Aces, one of the better teams in the Continental Basketball League. The others were former college and high school players. Rockwell had invited them to scrimmage the Big Reds.

Arch Thomas, one of Valley Falls High School's great players of former years, remembered Coach Rockwell's impact on his life and would go just about anywhere and do just about anything for his old coach. Standing six feet eight and weighing 240 pounds, Arch had been an All-American in college after graduating from Valley Falls High School. He'd once thought about quitting school when home pressures and falling grades had almost overwhelmed him. Rock simply wouldn't let him. Now, he was one of the league's outstanding centers.

Chip was sitting midway up the bleachers with Frank Watts and Herb Holden.

"Look at the size of them," Frank grimaced. "They make us look like a middle school team!"

"You're right about that," agreed Herb. "They're all good shots too."

Chip was excited. "Guess Coach wants to really find out how good we are!"

Just then Arch Thomas left his teammates, and three pairs of admiring eyes watched him leap lightly up the bleachers, three at a time, until he reached Rockwell's side. Rockwell and Arch engaged in earnest, animated conversation. From time to time, they gestured toward Taps Browning, who was deftly moving under the north basket, pulling down rebounds, and occasionally trying his pivot move.

"He must outweigh Taps more than fifty—sixty—pounds," Herb ventured, precisely voicing Chip's thoughts, "and he's at least four inches—"

"Can't be," interrupted Chip. "Taps is six-seven!"

"Well, looks like he'd make two of him anyway," persisted Frank. "But, remember—the biggest guy falls the hardest."

"Yeah, as long as they don't fall on *you!*" joked Herb.

The official's whistle ended all activity on the floor. Just like Rock, Chip was thinking, everything had to be just so. The scoreboard had to be operating and everything run just like a regular game including two offi-cials. *Hope the team makes a good showing . . . won't have to worry about Speed and Mike and Red. But this isn't three-man basketball. Like Coach had said in that first meeting, "Today's basketball can't be played with five men. You need players to come off the bench to make a team successful!"*

Chip wore no sweats today, but maybe he could work out later.

Coach Rockwell talked with the two officials in the center of the floor. As Rock left the court, the referee's whistle indicated it was time to start the scrimmage.

The visitors lined up quickly and confidently. Arch Thomas took a position outside the center circle, facing the south basket, and began talking to the referee who was holding the ball.

Valley Falls's Big Reds surrounded Coach Rockwell for his last-minute instructions. Chip moved close. He was curious about that fifth starter: would it be Pat, Lefty, or Soapy? Coach Rockwell was speaking. "Speed, you act as captain. Red and Mike at the guards. Taps at center." Then clearing his throat, the coach looked at lit-tle Pat Sanders and clasped him softly on the shoulder. "You go in at the other forward, Pat."

He extended his right hand, and the five starters placed their hands on his as he continued, "We'll play this practice game just like we play a regular game—for keeps! Let's go!"

The team dashed out on the floor amid shouts of encouragement from the bench.

"Let's go!"

"Pour it on 'em, guys!"

"What d'ya say, Valley Falls! What d'ya say!"

The official tossed the ball in the air, and the scrimmage was under way. Big Arch Thomas leaped forward and upward with the whistle, and the resulting contact completely spoiled Taps's jump. Before Browning even regained his balance, Thomas cut by him and, receiving a return pass from number 10, dribbled to the right of the south basket. As Mike switched to cover him, Thomas bounce-passed to his little forward, number 23, who neatly dropped the ball in the basket for the first score.

The visitors dominated the first half. Their superior height and weight precluded any effective Valley Falls play under either basket. Taps was buffeted right and left, and it was only through the jump shot efforts of Red and Mike that Valley Falls scored at all.

Lefty Peters took Mike's place for the last six minutes of the half and looked good, making two baskets on fast-break plays with Speed and Red.

Speed kept the defense from falling apart by daring interceptions, but at the end of the first half, the scoreboard showed Visitors 38, Valley Falls 19.

"Man, are they *good*," exclaimed Frank, moving close to Chip's side as they followed Chet Stewart and the team into the dressing room.

"How you gonna play clean against those guys?" demanded Pat pugnaciously, glaring around the room at the discouraged faces of his teammates. "They grab your arms and shove—"

"Be quiet!" bellowed Chet Stewart menacingly from his position by the door. "Sit down and keep quiet! No one talks in here except the coach!"

When Coach Rockwell entered the room a few seconds later, Chip got set for the explosion. This should be good; the guys had it coming. He laid the scorebook on the table and moved away.

"All right," Coach Rockwell began, studying some scribbled notes on a small card, "all right now—we haven't much time to talk nor much to talk about." Then, looking at Speed, he startled everyone as he exploded, "A fine captain! They run your team into the ground and no time-outs, no change of defense, no holding the ball on offense! Nothing! You changed nothing! They had and kept control of the game while we did nothing to stop their momentum."

Without waiting for an answer, Rockwell pointed an accusing finger at Browning. His words clicked like a computer keyboard plied by the fastest fingers. "Taps? Taps? TAPS? How'd you ever get that name? You haven't even *seen* the ball, much less *tapped* it! Taps, huh?" His voice was scornful and bitter as he continued, "You're so scared of Thomas you would jump over the basket if he yelled boo!"

For a long minute there wasn't a sound in the room. Chip was all confused. *What's with Coach?* He'd expected the coach to jump on the team, but Speed had been playing his head off, and Taps . . . why, Taps had been covered by two and sometimes three of the men every time he got near the basket. What did Rock expect?

"If I have to run this team from the bench, I'll do it! Now pay attention!" Moving to the strategy board, a miniature replica of the playing court, which Stewart had set up on the table, Rockwell placed the player pieces in a 2-1-2 zone formation.

"We'll try the 2-1-2 zone. Why, Red?"

"That'll do it, Coach," Schwartz nodded eagerly. "I was thinking about that a minute ago. The zone will keep those big guys away from the basket."

"What do you think, Speed?" Coach Rockwell looked at Morris intently as he waited.

"It's the right strategy, Coach. I must have been asleep, but I thought you'd tell me if you wanted me to make any changes."

"On the floor the captain's the boss," said Rockwell. "It takes brains to win games, and a smart, thinking captain doesn't wait for a letter from the coach before making a decision. I told you to act as captain—and I expect action! Right?"

Speed nodded firmly as Coach Rockwell shifted the pieces to the other end of the strategy board and continued, "On the offense, we'll fast-break every time—*every* time, you hear!—and if we can't beat them down with the break, we'll set up the horseshoe and draw those big, slow fellows out from under the basket and then outrun them. You're faster and younger! Understand, Browning?"

"Yes, Coach," Taps clipped through set jaws. "I guess I was foolish to try to score from underneath against all that height. They slapped away every shot I tried!"

"All right! We'll start the same five. And don't forget—they have a big lead, which means we've got to get that ball. Let's go!"

The second half was different. Either the change of tactics and continuous pressure Valley Falls kept on the visitors were getting results, or the men had tired and were coasting. Chip couldn't tell which. At any rate, Mike and Red were hitting from outside, and Speed and Pat were cutting around Taps for basket after basket. After another eight minutes, the score stood Visitors 46, Valley Falls 34. Arch Thomas called time-out and went into a huddle.

Coach Rockwell substituted Lefty Peters for Pat "Sandman" Sanders, and the game continued. It was just the same, except now Taps was setting up a post at the free-throw line and, after feeding Speed and Lefty as they cut by, was pivoting around Thomas and getting an inside position on the big center under the basket. With six minutes left to play, he scored three quick baskets, and the score stood Visitors 54, Valley Falls 51. The men again called time.

Coach Rockwell then sent Soapy Smith, the two Scott twins, Lefty Peters, and Bill English in to finish out the game. The men seized the opportunity to put on a freeze, passing the ball from one man to another without trying to shoot, and the scrimmage ended without further scoring. Final score: Visitors 54, Valley Falls 51.

As the players left the floor, Arch Thomas and Coach Rockwell sat down together on the home bench.

"What do you think, Arch?" asked Rockwell.

"First five look good, Coach," the big center said seriously, "but the subs are plenty weak."

"Yep, that's the score as we see it too."

Arch Thomas shook his head soberly and looked his former coach and mentor in the eyes. "Looks like you've got a rough season ahead, Coach."

Coach Rockwell seemed lost in thought but finally remarked, "Doesn't seem possible the alumni game's only a week away. Will you be with us?"

"Sure will! Couldn't keep me away!"

"What about Jacob Browning, Arch? Think he's got what it takes?"

"Yes, I do."

"He didn't look very good that first half."

Thomas grinned, "Well, Coach, you said to put the pressure on him. And that's what we did! He took everything we gave him that first half without much of an argument, but he was sure different in the second half."

"Browning is Chip Hilton's protégé. Chip's been working with him by the hour."

"Too bad you don't have Hilton this year, Coach. He's about the best high school player I ever saw!"

"He's that, all right! But you know, Arch, that Browning kid has great possibilities. All he needs is a little confidence."

"Well, I can take care of that, Coach. I'll see he gets some—in the alumni game!"

CHAPTER 12

The Alumni Game

THE ALUMNI game did not count in the season's record, but it was important to everyone—important to Coach Rockwell's coaching because it gave his team game practice, to the students because they could get a preseason view of the team and enjoy the dance following the game, and to the alumni because they could meet old friends and see the new kids.

Chip's pregame duties kept him as busy as Pop Brown! Chip got the roll of tickets, the ticket-seller's change, and the money box and ensured that the box office and the gate attendants were all set. He was apprehensive about this part of the manager's job because he was responsible for making sure the money and the unsold tickets were turned over to Burrell Rogers after the game.

Later, Chip helped Pop and Chet in the dressing room, checked the big scoreboard, and helped equip the alumni players. Now, satisfied that he'd completed his pregame duties, he sat at the scorer's table, hands under his chin, elbows resting on Valley Falls's brand-new scorebook. In a few minutes, the Big Reds would open their new basketball season.

Electing the captain of the varsity basketball team just before the first game of the season was a proud Valley Falls tradition and explained why Coach Rockwell and Chet Stewart were not in the dressing room with the team. Coach Rockwell always sat with the alumni and coached the old-timers. The newly elected captain was expected to take charge of the varsity.

With suspense, Chip watched the hall leading to the Valley Falls dressing room. There was no question in his mind who would be this year's basketball captain, but he could never tell for sure. If he were in that locker room right now, maybe there would be a scramble between him and Speed for the honor. Speed and Chip had been co-captains of the football team. They might even have been elected co-captains of the basketball team; that would have been something—best friends and co-captains in two sports.

Coach Rockwell always delegated Pop to stay with the team before the first game and to pass out little slips of paper for the athletes' votes. Chip could still remember last year when they had elected Butch Regan. It wouldn't be long now!

Chip shifted his eyes as a round of applause greeted Arch Thomas and the other alumni. Arch dribbled the ball down to the south basket and slammed it through the hoop. The crowd whooped in loud approval!

Then there was the expectant hush that always preceded the entrance of the Big Reds. Every eye focused on the doorway through which this year's new captain would lead the Valley Falls hopefuls.

THE ALUMNI GAME

Suddenly a tremendous cheer reverberated against the ceiling as Speed Morris, head down and dribbling the ball with fierce pride in his team, dashed out the door and headed for the north basket. No doubt about who was the leader of this team!

The Big Reds' energy electrified the crowd watching the spirited red-and-white-clad figures dash under the basket and back up the floor so fast it was hard to follow the ball. They were dynamos!

With the shrill of the official's whistle, the players began to strip off their warm-ups. Arch Thomas, Butch Regan, and the rest of the alumni starting five talked to Rock, firmly settled on the end of their bench. Speed, standing in front of the varsity bench, was soon joined by Red Schwartz, Taps Browning, Mike Rodriguez, and Pat Sanders. The tension was terrific.

Chip hadn't expected to feel this way and was surprised when he experienced that numb, trancelike, pregame hypnosis that all athletes feel just before the kickoff in football, the first pitch in baseball, or the opening toss in basketball. A sinking sensation filled the pit of his stomach, and something pounded at his chest. He could hardly breathe. Then the referee tossed the ball into the air, and it was all forgotten: the game was on!

Arch Thomas outjumped Taps and drove hard for the basket. Taps swung about almost in midair and was right behind Thomas, his hands waving. Chip's chest swelled with pride; Taps was fighting back.

Taps had jumped too quickly, but Chip was sure the rookie's overexcitement had ended after that first jump. The old-timers began to move the ball here and there, trying to find an opening. Then the ball was passed to Thomas, who head-and-shoulder-faked Taps out of position, pivoted, and scored. The alumni led by two points!

Chip watched Speed and Red. The sureness in their play was not evident in the running and passing of Mike and Pat. Speed and Red were completely relaxed, but there was a noticeable change of pace when they were forced to team up with one of the others.

Taps Browning stood on the free-throw line, back to the basket, feeding his teammates with the same passes he had practiced so faithfully in Chet Stewart's wall drill. Red Schwartz scored the first Valley Falls basket on a beautiful back bounce pass. The score was tied at two all.

Chip was thinking about Taps. This game would probably be the best test he would have all year. Arch Thomas was undoubtedly far superior to any high school player Taps would have to face. So far as that was concerned, thought Chip, Thomas was probably the best center Taps would ever face.

Toward the end of the first half, the alumni slowed down noticeably. Conditioning—rather a lack of it—was beginning to tell. The half ended with the score 26-22 in favor of the alumni.

The second half was no contest. Speed and Red scored almost at will, and Chip was so busy with his scorebook that he hardly saw the game as the varsity ran up the score to win, 66-45. Valley Falls had its first victory of the season!

The Valley Falls gymnasium could seat three thousand spectators. It had been filled to capacity on this first night, and now as the crowd started home, all but two people were talking about Valley Falls's basketball team.

Wheels Ferris wanted to talk about the game, but Joel Ohlsen's mood remained sullen, and he stalked along silently. When the two teenagers arrived at their corner, Wheels asked, "Going on home or going down to Mike's?"

"I'm not going down to Mike's. Wish I'd *never* gone there."

"What's the matter, Joel?"

"I'm in trouble, Wheels. Big trouble!"

"What kind of trouble?"

"Oh, I got in a mess down at the poolroom."

"What kind of mess? What d'ya do?"

"I got into a game with some men," Fats said miserably.

"At Sorelli's?"

"No, after Sorelli closed up. I went off with some men to play cards, and then we got into a dice game."

"So what happened?" Wheels persisted, looking sideways at Ohlsen.

"I lost a lot of money—more money than I ever had in all my life."

"Wait, man, you're losing me. If you didn't have the cash, how could you lose it?"

"I gave them a couple of checks."

"OK. So they cash the checks, and you just stay away from them, Joel."

"But I *haven't* got the money, Wheels," Joel said desperately. "Don't you understand? I don't have that much money in my account in the bank. I had the checkbook, so I wrote the checks just to get out of there. I lost nearly a thousand dollars."

"A thousand dollars?"

"Yes, and I don't know where I'm going to get it."

"You mean you wrote some checks, and you don't have the money to cover them?"

"That's right!"

"But, but—that's not allowed! I mean, it's like against the law, isn't it? Why'd you ever do that, Joel?"

"Why'd I *do* it? Why does anyone *do* stupid things like that? I only had a few bucks, and I lost that, and then they let me borrow some money, and I lost that. So I wrote the checks."

"What are you going to do now? What if they put the checks in the bank?"

"They said they'd hold them—until I could get the money—but I don't know where in the world I can get nearly a thousand dollars!"

"Who were these guys?" asked Wheels.

"That Smitty something and a big guy called Ed. I don't even know their last names."

"Didn't you write their names on the checks?"

"No, I made 'em out to cash. What am I going to do, Wheels?"

Later, as Wheels walked down the dark street that led to the flats, he thought desperately of some way to help his friend. Wheels had often daydreamed of the time when Joel Ohlsen would need him and he'd be able to show his loyalty. Well, here it was—and he couldn't do a thing.

A thousand dollars was a lot of money. It was more money than Wheels had ever seen. He knew it was probably more money than his other friends had combined. Certainly, his parents wouldn't give it to him. He didn't have an answer for Joel. It wasn't right; Joel had been tricked out of the money. But if J. P. Ohlsen ever heard about this, Joel would really be in trouble!

CHAPTER 13

Freeze the Ball

A SERIOUS group of teenagers watched the sports talk show in the Hilton family room a week later. The TV sports announcer was summarizing the high school basketball games of the past week while video clips of games were shown.

"Last year's champs, Weston, are continuing their winning ways. Definitely looks as if they're the team to beat for championship honors. The same five boys who walked off the court up at the university last March with the big trophy walked away with their third straight victory of the current season Wednesday night at Parkton, 44-39. That's the thirty-fourth consecutive win for the Cardinals.

"And last year's great runner-up team, the Stratford Indians, loaded with veterans, seems to be heading straight for this year's finals. The Stratford team annihilated the Salem Sailors, 52-31.

CHAMPIONSHIP BALL

"Down at Valley Falls, the Big Reds got off to a bad start—losing to Batson's zone, 54-45. Batson's zone defense completely dominated the game. Coach Henry Rockwell has only three holdovers from last year's regulars, which may account for the home-court defeat. That Batson zone made most of them look bad though—veterans or not.

"Over at Steeltown, the story was different. The Iron Men won two games this past week and ran their string to four in a row. Steeltown got off to an early start this year. Looks like they'll be one of the strong teams of the state. Over at Dane—"

Speed had seen enough. He reached out and turned off the TV. He was downcast. "How's your ankle, Taps?" he asked.

"No good." Taps stood up, tried a step or two, and then limped over to the couch and slumped down dejectedly.

"How'd it happen?" Speed was puzzled about Taps's injury.

"Just turned it—that's all."

"Don't see how you could have done it, Taps. I never knew anyone else to turn an ankle after Pop taped it."

"Coach see it?" asked Red.

"Not until after the game."

"Hope it's OK for the Parkton game," Red whispered.

"It will be!" Taps was determined.

"We might have won the Batson game anyway," Red said, "if Coach hadn't taken Sandman out."

"Coach couldn't leave him in," Chip broke in. "You know that! Coach isn't going to let anybody talk to the officials except Speed, and Pat's been told that a half-dozen times!"

"I know, Chip," said Speed. "But Pat's been having a lot of trouble, and he's all upset. You know what else he's doing—"

"Let's skip that!" suggested Chip.

"Live and learn," said Red, shrugging his shoulders.

"Live and lose when you don't learn, you mean," corrected Speed.

Red changed the subject, "Coach sure hates that Batson zone."

"Yeah, but we shoulda knocked them off, Red," Speed said.

"But Rock said it was his fault we lost."

"Look, Red," Speed continued, "you know it wasn't Rock's fault as much as I know it wasn't Rock's fault. We never lost to Batson at home before, and they've always used a zone. We just didn't have it together! We never did get organized. Well, I gotta go home. Ready to go, Red?"

As soon as the door closed, Chip turned to Taps, eyeing him directly, "Now, give me the lowdown, Taps. What's the real score about that ankle?"

"Well, Chip, Pop didn't tape my ankle the other night, but it was my fault. Guess I was too excited to ask him, and after I turned it, I didn't want to tell Coach 'cause I figured Pop would get the blame."

Chip nodded his head. "That's just what I figured. But Chet Stewart's just as much responsible for checking the ankles as Pop." He stopped suddenly. "Hey! So am I! I never thought of that!"

"It wasn't anyone's fault but mine," Taps said firmly. "I was one of the first dressed, but everyone was so busy and so rushed, I thought I'd let it go just that one time."

"One time—" Chip was thoroughly aroused now. "We've got to get that ankle taken care of right away. I'll call Doc Jones! Where's his number? Wait, I've got it!"

He dialed the number and waited impatiently until Jones answered. "Hello, Doc? This is Chip Hilton. Yes!

Doc, I hate to call you this time of night, but I wonder if you could do me a favor and come over and look at Taps's ankle. . . . Yes, Taps Browning. Yes, he turned it the other night in the Batson game. . . . You will? Thanks!"

Chip hung up the phone. "He's coming right over, Taps. I sure hope he can fix it up for the Parkton game. The whole season just about depends on you!"

In the days that followed, Taps's ankle improved a little, but he was still limping when the Big Reds lined up for the Parkton game. Parkton's Coach Robbins had realized his young and inexperienced players couldn't keep pace with Valley Falls in scoring. So he had instructed them to hold the ball on the offense. He had figured a passing and stalling style might upset the classier Valley Falls team, and this was exactly what was happening.

Lefty Peters, Mike Rodriguez, and Taps couldn't take it. They were lunging at the ball, trying to intercept passes and providing a perfect reaction to Coach Robbins's strategy. As soon as Speed realized Parkton's objective, he called for a time-out. In the huddle he laid down the law. "You guys have to play a careful game," he said. "This bunch isn't going to run with us. We've been playing right into their hands. We're going to hold that ball too. Now don't forget—Lefty, Mike, Taps—make good, solid passes. They can't beat us as long as we have the ball! Move it around and let Red and me take the chances. Understand? Got it?"

At the end of the first half, the boys filed into the dressing room without a word. Coach Rockwell studied the scorebook and then turned his attention to the shot chart. Herb Holden and Frank Watts were responsible for these stats. Coach Rockwell knew the information compiled on the shot charts was extremely valuable. The shot charts were printed replicas of a basketball court done to scale. The number of every player who attempted a goal was jotted down on the chart as close as possible to the exact spot from where the shot was taken. If the shot was successful, the player's number was circled. Herb Holden's job went even further. He was supposed to list all assists and the number of offensive and defensive rebounds for each player. Turnovers because of bad passes, interceptions, and dribbling were included. In the hall outside Coach Rockwell's office hung a big chart, the Player Performance Chart, which listed each player and recorded his performance for all games to date. After each game, the information contained on the game charts was transferred to the large chart outside Rockwell's door. Anyone could look at this chart and tell almost at a glance which players were important in the games played so far.

Coach Rockwell stepped in front of the two rows of benches; the players were all at attention. Even though they were behind in the score, they could sense Rock was satisfied with their play during the half. "Boys," he began, "this is a game that can be easily lost. We've got to be careful. I wasn't surprised that you were a bit upset at first, but you're playing well now. When Speed took that time-out and told you just what Parkton was trying to do, I wondered if you could pull yourselves together and play smart. Bill Robbins is a clever coach. I had dinner with him last night, and he never said a thing about pulling this little surprise. Just what is their strategy, Red?"

"It's just like Speed said in the huddle, Coach. He said they were freezing the ball and trying to get us so upset we'd lose our heads. Speed told us not to try to force a score but to pass the ball around until we got a good shot."

"That's right, Red, but that's not the whole story. Is it, Speed?"

"Not by a long shot, Coach. We've got it all over Parkton as far as passing and shooting are concerned. They're an inexperienced team. They don't have anybody back from last year. They want to keep the score close and then in the last few minutes of the game, they'll start firing those shots up! Then if they get hot—good-bye, Valley Falls!"

"That's right." Coach Rockwell was nodding his head. "If they get hot and happen to hit with a few quick shots, and you guys get excited and miss, you're going to lose a game everybody expects you to win."

Striking the table with his fist, he emphasized each word: "I want you to get that ball! And when you get it, keep it until you get a good shot under the basket. The first player who takes a foolish shot is going to come out of the game—and stay out! We've got to play this one smart. Keep in mind you're three points behind. That means you've got to play heads-up on defense. You'll get ahead—I know that, but not by taking risky shots. Understand? Lefty? Mike? Taps? All right then!" The boys listened intently as Coach Rockwell went on.

"Now, when we get ahead, we'll use the freeze." He turned to the board and quickly drew the outline of the front half of a court. He explained that the Big Reds must be sure to get the ball across the division line in ten seconds and be sure to stay in the frontcourt. If they stepped on the center line or the sideline, they'd lose the ball.

"And be careful of your passes. Keep the ball moving and keep moving yourself. No dribbling. Keep spread

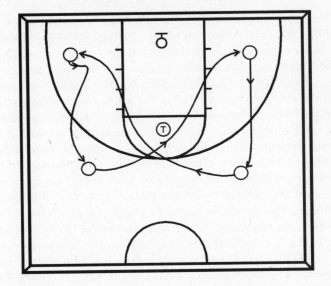

out. Remember, they'll be out to steal the ball, and they'll double up on you if you don't keep moving.

"Taps, *be sure* you stand just above the free-throw line." Rockwell turned to the board and placed a T in the semicircle near the free-throw line. "Be careful—don't let either foot touch the free-throw line or the three-second rule will be in effect and we might turn the ball over.

"Follow the paths shown on the board, and I want every player to come out and meet the ball—come toward your teammate to receive the ball. No blind passes! Now, Speed, you've got two time-outs left. Use them if you need them. In that last quarter, if we get ahead—which we will—we're going to freeze the ball right up to the horn. Understand? We'll give Bill Robbins a little taste of his own medicine!"

CHAMPIONSHIP BALL

All heads were nodding. The players could see now what the coach had meant by playing with their heads. There was more to basketball than passing, dribbling, and shooting. No wonder there were so many upsets in basketball. An unfamiliar offense or defense, or a strategy such as Parkton was using tonight, might change the game's tempo and easily upset the best team in the state.

Chip glanced down at Taps's ankle. Taps caught his eye and shook his head almost imperceptibly. His ankle was troubling him. Chip had noticed it in the first half. Parkton's style had made it easier on Taps since he hadn't been forced to do much running. If Coach Robbins found out that Taps had a bad leg, the Parkton center might run him into the ground and out of the game.

The second-half tempo sped up a bit, but at the end of the third quarter Parkton was still leading. Taps had been going from bad to worse. The Parkton center had discovered that Taps was hurt and was running rings around him.

Shortly after the fourth period started, Coach Rockwell removed Taps from the game. There was only a slight spatter of applause for the big center who had looked so flat. Taps had tried to keep from limping, and the fans didn't know he had a bad ankle; they thought he was being outplayed. Bill English reported for Taps. He and the Parkton center were about the same size.

Now the VF fans were impatient; the end of the game was in sight, and Valley Falls was down by one point. The Big Reds had to go ahead soon if they were going to win this game! Speed and Red were trying to set up their favorite give-and-go play. They maneuvered slowly and carefully.

Suddenly, Speed cut in front of Red, changed direction, and cut hard for the basket. Red lobbed a high pass over the head of Speed's guard, who was trailing the speedster in his sudden dash for the goal. It seemed as if the ball was going clear out of bounds, but at the last second, Speed leaped high in the air and grasped the ball with his left hand. His body seemed to hang in space as he tried to get control of the ball.

With a desperate twist of his body, Speed squared up and neatly kissed a soft shot off the glass backboard, and the ball fell cleanly through the hoop. Valley Falls was in the lead for the first time in the game by one thin point. The crowd went wild!

Speed immediately called time out, and Rockwell substituted the Scott brothers for Mike Rodriguez and Lefty Peters. Matt and Ryan were expert passers and dribblers but poor shots. The Rock's strategy was obvious to every player on the bench; now it would be the Big Reds' turn to hold the ball if they could get it before Parkton could score.

Parkton brought the ball up the court carefully—too carefully. The Parkton players were tight and jittery. Speed seemed to be out on his feet. He moved slowly and with apparent effort. He leaned slightly forward, holding his side with one hand, breathing in short, quick gasps through parted lips.

Chip had seen Speed pull this trick many times; behind this feigned exhaustion lay a hawklike concentration. Then a Parkton player fell for the fake. He threw a cross-court pass toward Speed's opponent, but the ball never reached its mark. Speed shot forward like a streak of lightning, intercepted the ball, and dribbled for the basket. He might have scored, but he didn't try it. His opponent was right on his heels as Speed circled back from the basket and continued the dribble.

CHAMPIONSHIP BALL

Only a minute of play remained, and now Parkton got a dose of its own medicine. Valley Falls was freezing the ball perfectly. Closer and closer, the Parkton players pressed, but Matt, Ryan, Red, and Speed were passing beautifully.

Then, Bill English brought dismay to every Valley Falls supporter in the gym—he ran into a Parkton player. Bill had tried to keep out of the way but collided with an opponent, and a foul was called against him. A Parkton player shooting free throws *was not* what Valley Falls needed now—especially with Valley Falls committing its seventh foul of the half.

As the players moved down the floor to the Parkton basket, Coach Rockwell sent Soapy Smith in for English. The move surprised Soapy and everyone else. Soapy was the slowest man on the team.

The crowd was deathly quiet as the Parkton center moved to the free-throw line. Scarcely pausing, he dropped both shots cleanly through the net—Parkton was in the lead by one point!

Thirty seconds left to play—Valley Falls's ball. Speed passed to Red—Red to Matt—Matt to Ryan—then over to Speed, who glanced at the clock and dribbled toward the corner. Soapy was sliding back and forth directly under the basket trying to gain a good pivot position.

Chip was thinking how many times he had maneuvered for a good pivot position under the basket. Those long hours of practice under the old hoop at home had contributed to making him the highest scorer in the state. But Soapy was too slow.

Speed was standing still now—holding the ball and looking up at the big clock. When it showed seven seconds to play, he faked a drive for the basket and hooked the ball to Soapy—hoping to get a return pass for a drive to the basket. Instead, Soapy took the ball high in the air for a shot, but before he had a chance to release the ball, the Parkton center fouled him.

There were less than four seconds left to play when Soapy walked to the foul line; he held the game in the palm of his hand.

Chip looked at Rockwell. If Coach could only substitute someone for Soapy now, but that couldn't be done. The rules didn't permit it.

Rockwell, seated on the bench, leaning forward, hands covering his face, looked steadily down at the floor. Soapy, standing at the free-throw line, turned toward the players on the bench and winked and grinned. Chip could have killed him!

The referee handed the ball to Soapy. Rockwell lifted his head slightly and peeked between his spread fingers.

Nonchalantly, as if the shot were of no importance, Soapy smiled once more toward the bench and bounced the ball three times on the floor. Then he winked confidently toward Coach Rockwell and proceeded to arch both shots right through the basket!

Parkton, after taking its last time-out, inbounded the ball but was checked by the blaring horn before getting off a desperation heave from the backcourt.

Valley Falls had defeated a weaker Parkton team by one point. Soapy's two free throws had made the winning difference!

The players on the floor and those on the bench mobbed him before he could move off the court. He was pounded on the back, shoved, slapped, and high-fived all the way to the locker room. But he didn't seem to mind; he kept grinning and asking, "Think the Rock'll let me shoot free throws for everyone from now on?"

CHAPTER 14

Coach Speaks His Mind

CHIP PAUSED outside Coach Rockwell's office. He had decided to tell the coach about Taps's ankle. He was busy thinking and absent-mindedly barged right into Coach Rockwell's office without knocking.

"I happen to know that his family is moving to town, Hank. What's more, I'm giving this kid's father a job." Jerry Davis, one of Valley Falls's staunchest sports fans, was speaking. Chip paused uncertainly.

Strained silence hung heavily in the room, and it was an embarrassed Hilton who finally blurted out, "Excuse me, Coach. I thought you were alone."

"That's all right, Chip. Come in and sit down."

"I can come back," Chip offered.

"No, sit down!" Rock seemed almost eager to have him there—as if he needed him.

Chip noted the Rock's set jaw and flushed face. Coach seemed pretty angry about something.

COACH SPEAKS HIS MIND

Jerry Davis cleared his throat. "This kid is really a center, Rock: six feet seven or eight, two hundred pounds, and moves like a streak. He's just the thing for us. I don't think you'll ever have a chance to get a natural like him again. And the way Speed, Red, and Mike are playing, he's a sure bet to put you into the tournament."

"Nope, can't be done!" Rock snapped decisively.

"Well, why not?"

"We've never admitted a boy here in the middle of the year and let him play varsity. It just can't be done!"

"But his parents are moving to town. If a family moves to a town and the boy is admitted regularly to school, he can play on any team he can make. The state athletic rules contain nothing that restricts a boy from competing under those circumstances."

Davis paused expectantly, but Coach Rockwell said nothing. "Look at Delford," continued Davis, "and their big center, Red Henry. He transferred there right in the middle of last year, and Jenkins played him."

"That's Delford, that's Jenkins, not Valley Falls!"

"Look at Rutledge. Burger, their big center, played three years at Cortley over in Ohio before he transferred—and he's playing! Nobody's kicking about that, and he's the most talked-about player in the state. Why, he's averaging twenty points a game!"

"Nope, it's still not the same. Burger started school at Rutledge in September. Why, is none of my business. If this boy—whatever his name is—had come here in September, OK. But nothing doing in the middle of the year."

"But I can't see what difference it makes if he wants to come. He's moving to town soon. The new term starts in February. His coach has already released him; he isn't even playing at his current school now."

"I'm not interested! If he wants to come here and go to school, OK. He can play next year. But we're not going to let any boy transfer here in the middle of the season and play basketball. That's final!"

"Well, you're the coach, but you're making a big mistake. If you use Myers, you'll be in the tournament by a mile. He gets better every game he plays! Wait and see. You're going to regret this!"

Chip wished he could tell them about Taps's ankle. If Coach thought he was "coming along," what would he think if he knew Taps had been playing all along with a bad ankle?

"But we need an experienced center," Davis persisted.

"Not that bad!"

"It happens every year. Why, it isn't fair to keep the boy from playing. There's no ruling that prohibits a kid from playing when his family moves to a town and he enters at the beginning of a term."

"OK, but it's not going to happen here. Besides, it would be getting around the very principle that led to the formation of the State Athletic Association."

"Well, then, Hank, why didn't they bar Krieger at Bloomfield?"

"I don't know, Jerry." Coach Rockwell stood up and moved toward the door. His attitude plainly expressed his lack of interest in further discussion. "Drop in again, sometime!"

"OK! I guess you know what you're doing. Hello, Hilton. So long, Hank."

Coach Rockwell swung around and looked at Chip. "How's it going?"

"Pretty good after that Parkton game, Coach."

"Yes, that gave us all a lift. You heard what Jerry Davis had to say about Taps Browning, didn't you?"

COACH SPEAKS HIS MIND

"Yes, I did, Coach, and—" Chip's thoughts flashed to Taps and his ankle. Davis thought Taps was going to be a flop. Maybe Coach did too. *Well, here goes . . . I might as well get it over with.*

"Coach, there's something you ought to know."

"What's that, Chip?"

"You know—you know about Taps's bad ankle?"

"Yes."

"Coach, Taps's ankle wasn't taped the night of the Batson game."

"What do you mean?"

"You see, Coach, I asked Taps the day after the Batson game what was wrong with his ankle, and he admitted he didn't get it taped."

"Why not?" Coach Rockwell bit off the words in a hard voice.

"Taps said he waited a long while, but everybody was so busy he didn't want to bother anyone. He didn't want to be the last one out on the floor either—so he let it go."

"A fine thing!" Coach Rockwell's face was flushed. "That's a fine thing! Chet's supposed to check all the ankles; Pop too. And by the way, what were you thinking about that night? You're supposed to help out too!"

"It was my fault, Coach. I should have thought about Taps before anybody else."

"A fine thing! No wonder the kid hasn't been able to play. Where's he now?"

"Probably down at the Sugar Bowl, Coach."

"Well, come along. We'll pick him up and go over to see Doc Jones."

Coach Rockwell's driving and general attitude plainly discouraged conversation.

A little later, they stood watching Doc Jones patiently examine Taps's ankle. "Yes, Hank, I know," said Doc Jones. "I took care of the ankle. It's coming along all right."

"Why didn't you tell me about it?" fumed the coach.

"There wasn't anything you could do, Hank. A sprained ankle is a sprained ankle. It takes time to heal!"

"I understand that, but what I don't understand is why I wasn't told about it. The school physician, Chet, Pop, Hilton, here—everyone knew about the ankle except me. I'm just the coach! I suppose I'll have to start taping ankles next!"

He glared at Browning. "Why didn't you tell me?" Without waiting for an answer, Rockwell turned back again to Doc Jones.

"Did you take an X-ray?" he asked.

"No. I didn't think it was necessary."

"Well, take one!" He paused at the door. "While you're at it, X-ray Hilton's ankle too. Let's see what that leg of his looks like." He closed the door with a crash, and Jones, Taps, and Chip all breathed a sigh of relief. But their relief didn't last long. The door was suddenly yanked open just enough to admit Coach Rockwell's head.

"X-ray their heads while you're at it too. Let me know what's rattling around up there!"

CHAPTER 15

Moral Responsibility

CHIP WALKED over to the corner of the school cafeteria where the athletes usually gathered and placed his tray on the table next to Biggie Cohen's.

"Hey, Chip," Biggie said. Then, leaning close to Chip, he whispered, "I've got some bad news about Fats Ohlsen."

"What did you do—punch him?" Chip laughed.

"No, course not! His arrogant stupidity is catching up with him though, at last!"

"What happened?"

"Comin' to school this morning I met Wheels Ferris. He told me about a huge loss Fats took in a game with some men. Some of those sharpshooters who hang around Sorelli's took him for a lot of money."

Chip shrugged and said, "He can afford it."

"No, he can't! That's just the point. Wheels told me Fats didn't have the money and gave them some checks.

Said Fats is really scared and is thinking about leaving home, because he doesn't have any money in the bank."

"How much did he lose?"

"Nearly a thousand dollars!"

"*A thousand dollars!*" Chip's mouth fell open, and he gazed at Biggie in amazement. "A thousand dollars," he repeated slowly.

"That's what Wheels said. Wheels wants you and me to see the Rock and get him to straighten it out."

"Wants you and me to see Rock?" Chip stared at Biggie incredulously "*You* and *me?* Feeling the way we do? That's the best one yet. As if he's got a real chance of that happening!"

"I know, Chip. I felt that way too, but I've been thinking it over all morning. Guess I've got plenty reason to hate that guy, but there's more to this than Fats Ohlsen."

"I can't see it," Chip shook his head. His lips were set in a thin, straight line. "Why doesn't Wheels go see the coach himself?"

"He's afraid Fats will get mad at him. Look, Chip, Fats Ohlsen means nothing to me. Never did care for the guy, but something's got to be done about those gamblers down there. They never work. They just hang around and take money away from a lot of the hard-working pottery guys who can't afford it. Besides, lots of the younger kids here in school think they're cool! Some of the guys even try to dress like 'em. Somebody's got to do something about it, and the Rock's the one person who can do it! He hates that whole group."

"They ought to close the place," Chip muttered.

"How about us seeing Rockwell?" Biggie persisted.

Chip shrugged his shoulders. "I'll go along, but I don't know if I feel too good about it."

MORAL RESPONSIBILITY

Coach Rockwell greeted Biggie and Chip with a smile. "Well, what brings you two around here at lunch hour? Good to see you, Biggie. Where've you been keeping yourself?"

"Working and studying, Coach. Don't need a good standing guard, do you?"

Coach Rockwell shook his fist at Biggie and smiled. "I thought we decided two years ago that," he paused and winked at Chip before continuing, "as a basketball player, you're a pretty good tackle."

"Thanks for the compliment, Coach," Biggie laughed.

"You don't do bad in baseball though, Biggie. Now what's on your mind?"

Coach Rockwell soon knew the whole story. He sat in silence for a long time before speaking. "I don't know whether this situation is any of your business—or mine. I've warned all you kids many times to stay away from that place. Other students too. Of course, Ohlsen hasn't been out for athletics since I bounced him off the football squad last fall. I haven't had much chance to talk to him about his personal life since we had to part company. I doubt whether he would like my butting in on his private problems now. Yet, I do think his father should know."

"Don't do that, Coach!" Biggie was distressed. "I promised Wheels I would tell only you and Chip about it."

"How about those fellows who hang around the poolroom—they all know about it, don't they?"

"I don't think so, Coach. Anyway, they wouldn't want J. P. to know about it any more than Fats would. J. P. would probably run a campaign and close the place. They sure don't want that!"

Coach Rockwell rubbed his ear vigorously. "OK, you boys let me see what I can do." After the two friends had gone, Rockwell thumped his desk with a heavy fist. "That's the trouble with some people," he growled aloud, "spoiling their kids with a lot of money. No boy should have money unless he earns it himself. Then he'd learn how to take care of it!"

Late that night, Coach Henry Rockwell paid a visit to Sorelli's. Mike Sorelli looked up in surprise. He had been one of the supporters of the veteran coach for many years. But this was the first time Rockwell had ever been in his business. Rockwell glanced quickly back along the chairs lining the walls and then at the clock. It was 11:30.

"Why, hello, Coach. Don't tell me you want to play a game of pool?"

"No, Mike, I don't want to play pool. I came down here tonight to see you about something much more important."

"What is it, Coach? You can count on me!"

"I hope I can. You know Joel Ohlsen, I guess."

"You mean Fats Ohlsen? Sure! Why?"

"Only one reason—and I think you know it. Some of the low-lifes who hang out here took that boy for nearly a thousand dollars, and he gave them some checks. He doesn't have the money. I want you to get those checks, Mike."

"Now wait a minute, Coach. That's none of my business. I don't allow gambling in my place. If Fats Ohlsen got mixed up with some gamblers, you can't hold me responsible."

"But they hang out here, Mike. And this is where they made up the deal."

"Fats Ohlsen is big enough to take care of himself!"

"True enough, Mike, but not *old* enough. I expect you to get those checks. If you don't, you're going to be in for a lot of trouble."

MORAL RESPONSIBILITY

"But what have I got to do with it, Coach? Fats Ohlsen comes in here to play pool. So what? No one ever plays cards or shoots dice in my place, and *I* don't gamble—"

"The men who took those checks come in here," interrupted Rockwell, "and a lot of high school kids come in here too. Those men knew they were playing with a kid, and both you and I know they don't have any business gambling with youngsters."

"Look, Coach, I heard something about it, but it's none of my business. But if you say so, I'll find out about it and let you know the score."

"I don't want to know the score. I want those checks!"

"What am I supposed to do—make up Fats Ohlsen's losses? I didn't have nothing to do with it!"

"Now you listen to me, Mike Sorelli. That game started right here in this poolroom. In the first place, you shouldn't let the kids hang out here. You've got the pottery workers coming in here regularly and that's enough! Those men work for their money and know how to take care of it. Maybe you don't want to keep this poolroom open. If you don't, then just keep on letting those characters who hang out here associate with high school kids."

"Look, Coach, you got it all wrong!"

"Mike, you know the type of fellow who mostly hangs out here better than I do. When they take advantage of a kid who meets them here, that makes it *your* responsibility!"

"Look, Coach!" Mike was desperate. "Look! I can't keep high school kids from walking in here. I never let 'em play in no games, Coach."

"They're not supposed to come in here, and playing has nothing to do with it."

"I know, Coach, but they'll think I'm picking on 'em." Mike was squirming. "Anyway, I don't have a legal right to keep 'em out!"

"That's true, Mike. No legal right! But you do have a moral right. Furthermore, I was always under the impression that you supported our high school's teams, that you knew that any boy who broke the rules would be dropped from the team, and that you knew that dropping a boy from a team often meant the ruination of a good season. Guess I must have been wrong about you, Mike!"

"No, you weren't, Coach! Honest! I'd do anything for the team—for you too, far's that's concerned. Whatever you say goes. I'll make a lot of enemies, I suppose. But from here on, the high school kids are gonna stay *out!*"

CHAPTER 16

The Missing Box

IT WAS the first practice day of the new term. Examinations were over, and report cards were out. Some members of the squad had slipped through by the skin of their teeth. But there was general rejoicing that the team remained intact despite every effort by a few members of the faculty. Everybody was feeling fine. There was considerable chatter and laughter and horseplay on the bleachers where Chip had gathered the squad.

Chip should have known by the stern look on Coach Rockwell's face when he came through the door that something grave had happened. Then the stunning blow fell.

"Sanders, turn in your uniform." The coach's words were spoken quietly and firmly.

Chip heard a gasp of surprise and dismay from the huddle of boys on the bleachers. He looked at Pat Sanders. The boy's face was as pale as death. A moment later, he was at the door. Chip caught a glimpse of his face as he clumsily reached for the handle. His eyes were blinded with tears. What had happened? Why, Pat had been the find of the season! He had been a sensation against Batson, and now with the Weston game only three days away, he was dropped from the squad!

Coach Rockwell shuffled his scouting notes and plunged right into a discussion of the game with Weston, as though nothing had happened.

"Now, boys, Weston uses a strict man-to-man defense. Not much switching. This Weston team doesn't have to switch much; they keep on top of you all the time. You're going to have to move against this team, or they'll put you in their back pockets.

"Hilton, I want you to take English this afternoon and coach him to play just like Fraling. You've played against Fraling several times, and you know all his moves. Make Bill do everything Fraling does.

"Matt and Ryan, you two are going to be Benson and Young." Coach Rockwell accentuated his words, tapping the marker on the board, as he continued. "Don't forget—these two players, along with Fraling, do nearly all the scoring for Weston. The other two men on their team stay out on top and keep the defense honest.

"Chet, take these boys out on the court and practice everything you and I discussed this morning. Chip, you concentrate on English. We've got to stop Fraling. As soon as you are sure English knows all of Fraling's stuff, Chet will put him against Browning. Taps, you go along with Hilton and English and watch everything they do."

Out on the court, Chip's thoughts jumped back to Sanders. How had Coach Rockwell found out about Pat?

THE MISSING BOX

Oh, no! The team might even think I told Coach. Pat is an OK guy, but he's been playing outside ball, all right. Some of the guys knew it; they figured he'd get caught. Well, there just wasn't any middle ground with the Rock. Sanders played outside ball, the coach found it out, and Pat was through.

For half an hour Chet Stewart worked with the players who represented the Weston team. Chip drilled Bill English over and over on all the moves the big Weston center was famous for. Chip knew Fraling inside and out. He had played against him as a sophomore, but Fraling had improved even more.

Taps followed every move and occasionally asked pertinent questions. Chip could hardly wait until he could get to work on Taps at home. Ankle or no ankle, Taps just had to turn in a good game Friday. Chip Hilton was assuming that responsibility.

Friday of that week was a night to be *long* remembered. There hadn't been a game like it in Valley Falls for years. It was a game for the record books—a game that would be talked about over and over again. Although the game had ended half an hour earlier, the crowd was still standing around in the gym and in the hallway. The fans just wouldn't go home. Every once in a while someone would let out a whoop, and then the whole crowd would start cheering again.

Valley Falls had beaten Weston! Yes, WESTON! The Cardinals! Undefeated for two straight years, Weston had lost to the Big Reds tonight chiefly because of the scoring of little Lefty Peters and the defensive play of big Taps Browning. Fraling, the Cardinals' center, hadn't scored a point! It was unbelievable!

In the hall, friends, parents, and students were waiting for their particular heroes to come out of the locker room. It was a great night!

Coach had grabbed Chip as soon as he entered the room. "Nice going! Taps told me about those home practice sessions you and he went through to stop Fraling. You sure did it, kid!"

"I didn't do anything, Coach. Taps—"

Coach Rockwell never heard him. He had moved away and was slapping Taps on the back and yelling something to Speed. Speed had Lefty by the hair. "That's what he did," he yelled. "He scalped 'em!"

"One-handed too," someone hollered.

"Yeah, left-handed," yelled Speed.

Everyone had been worried when Coach Rockwell had dropped Pat Sanders, but tonight Lefty Peters had proved himself. Yes, Lefty had scored sixteen points and the winning basket with only seconds to go.

Soapy was repeating over and over, "That ball acted like it had eyes when Lefty shot it. Yes sir, it did have eyes!"

Yes, Valley Falls had beaten the great Weston team, state champions, undefeated for thirty-eight games. The Big Reds had beaten the Cardinals 42-41, on Lefty's last-minute baseball throw from the Valley Falls backcourt, and because Taps Browning had played unbelievable defensive basketball and scored five baskets and two free throws to take second place in the scoring with twelve points.

"Nah, that last basket was lucky," Lefty kept saying. Coach Rockwell had used only six players in the game. Morris, Browning, Schwartz, Rodriguez, and Peters had started the game. These five had played the full thirty-two minutes, except for Morris, who had been relieved by Soapy Smith for less than a minute midway in the final quarter. Up to then, Morris, Schwartz, and Rodriguez had been bottled up completely. Between them, they had made only fourteen points.

Coach Rockwell and Morris had stood on the sidelines briefly, and then Speed had dashed back into the game to call a time-out and instruct the Valley Falls five to freeze the ball the last minute of play if they were ahead. However, Weston had taken the lead seconds later, and it was the Cardinals who tried to hold the ball the last minute of play. Five seconds before the end of the game, Lefty Peters had intercepted a Weston pass and, standing way in the backcourt, had thrown the ball like a baseball for the basket. Everyone knew the rest—the ball had smacked loudly against the backboard and had incredibly dropped through the hoop.

Carrying the metal box that contained the gate receipts, Chip was stopped in the hall by *Yellow Jacket* reporters who wanted to look at the scorebook. He placed the cash box on the table and soon became completely engrossed in answering their questions and explaining the symbols that described the game.

Some time later, Chip picked up the scorebook and started toward the locker room. Then he remembered the cash box. He had forgotten it! He hurried back to the table, but the box wasn't there. It had disappeared! He told himself to calm down. Maybe he had left it in the box office, but, no, he remembered placing the box on the table in the hall.

The box office was closed, deserted. He barged upstairs to Rogers's office. Rogers wasn't there. Chip hurried back to the locker room and searched frantically through his locker, under the table, and in the big waste can. He rushed into Pop Brown's storeroom. Pop turned to Chip with startled eyes. "What's the matter, Chipper? What's going on?"

"The money box, Pop! The money box—it's gone!"

"Gone? Where?"

But Chip had hurried back upstairs and out into the gym. There wasn't a thing on the scorer's table. He glanced along the row of bleachers. Only a few enthusiastic fans remained. Looking beyond them, he noticed Rogers talking to Coach Rockwell near the door leading to the hall. He looked fearfully from one to the other, but there was no evidence of the box. He approached them with a tremendous fear in his heart. The box was gone! It definitely was gone!

A half-hour of futile searching by Rogers, Coach Rockwell, Chet Stewart, Pop Brown, building superintendent, Mr. Anderson, and Speed followed—but no box.

Two hours later, Chip and Speed started home. The silent ride was broken only by Speed's futile attempts to cheer up his friend. Chip had been thrilled beyond words—beyond thinking—by the great victory.

But he accused himself bitterly. There had been over fourteen hundred dollars in that box—*fourteen hundred dollars!*

A distraught boy tossed and turned all that night. He relived every second that had passed since he had placed the box on the table. Who had been in that crowd surrounding him and the *Yellow Jacket* reporters? Who could have taken the box? Even Coach Rockwell's encouraging comment, "Oh, it'll turn up in the morning," was no comfort.

And so Chip Hilton passed one of the bleakest nights of his young life.

CHAPTER 17

Everybody Loves a Winner!

COACH ROCKWELL had just finished taping a big red X on the gym floor to mark the spot of Lefty Peters's great shot when Chip hesitantly approached him. Sitting back on his haunches, the coach studied Chip, who nervously shifted his weight between his bad leg and his good one. He startled Chip with a sudden torrent of words. His words were like the clicking of an old typewriter: sharp, clear, and tumbling one over the other.

"Now you listen to me, young man! I won't have any more of this foolish talk. Everyone knows you're sorry. We all know you would like to make good the loss, pay it out of your Sugar Bowl wages. So what? Things like this happen many times during a coaching career.

"Don't you think Burrell Rogers and I know how to handle situations like this one? That's part of our jobs. We carry insurance for just such eventualities, and besides, the Athletic Association has enough money in the bank to take care of the lost money without any help from William Hilton!

"We've got to win *two* of the three games scheduled on the road trip, if we're going to go anywhere in our division. Maybe if you'll quit crying on everyone's shoulder about that stupid box, you'll have time to look after your manager's job and get things set right for the trip, as you should!"

Chip's face flushed and his eyes narrowed as Coach Rockwell's sharp words struck home. Then he caught the friendly glint in the watchful eyes. Chip's red deepened still further. What was the matter with him? Coach was needling him because he was acting like a wimp.

"I get it!" he said.

As they walked together toward the storeroom, Chip recalled the days that had passed since the Weston game. He hadn't been able to think about anything except the missing box. His mother had downplayed the loss: "Don't worry about it, Chip. We can pay it back—easily!" Coach was right; moping around wouldn't do any good. His thoughts were interrupted by the coach's voice.

"Managing's pretty tough, isn't it, kiddo?"

"Times like this it is," Chip smiled wryly. "Guess it isn't as hard as coaching though," he ventured.

"What makes you think coaching is so bad?"

"Well, it doesn't seem to be very much fun. When you win, they say you should have won by a larger score, and when you lose, you're really in trouble, and they all tell you how they would've won the game."

"Yes, but there're some compensations that more than make up for that."

"You mean the team, I bet."

EVERYBODY LOVES A WINNER!

"I sure do mean the team! Watching kids like you come along, develop initiative and courage and sportsmanship. Why, it's the best job in the world!"

Thursday morning, Chip jostled his way through the thick crowd in the school parking lot and joined Coach Rockwell, Chet Stewart, and the team.

"All set, Chip?"

"Everything's checked, Coach. I've got what we need."

The Big Reds were stowing bags, shedding coats, laughing, shouting, and talking. Chip sat with Taps. He felt good today. The bus moved quietly forward. They were on their way—on a trip that could make or break the chances for the Big Reds team.

Three days later, a jubilant Big Reds team was homeward bound once more. The trip, which had started off badly with the unexpected loss to Parkton by a 43-40 score, had wound up in a blaze of glory. Coach Rockwell was speaking excitedly. Yes, Coach was happy today! So was Chip—so was everybody! The Big Reds had won the last two games of the trip!

On Friday night they had taken Hampton, 49-46, and the very next night had beaten the Sailors, 51-42.

Chet Stewart, Chip, Red, Speed, and Taps were listening intently to Rockwell's words. "We learned something on this trip, Chet. Bill English proved a big man could be stopped from the front. Taps, you want to keep that in mind. Some of the big centers coming up may be a little too tough to play from the back."

"How about Delford's Red Henry?" inquired Chet.

"Right!" agreed the coach. "He's too big to play straight."

"Speed and Red sure had their eyes on the old hoop, didn't they, Coach?" Chip was beaming.

"And, don't forget those shots of Soapy's!" Speed interrupted. "Old Soapy's really got the jump shot down."

"He's coming along," agreed Coach Rockwell. "Wonder how he developed it so fast?"

Speed laughed. "Soapy didn't develop it! Soapy didn't develop anything! Chip's responsible. He's had Soapy over behind the house every day, even out in the rain, and then he takes Soapy up to the Y every night for an hour."

"Yeah, and every Saturday, too," added Red Schwartz.

"A good thing we had Soapy along," Chet Stewart nodded gratefully.

"He was great!" added Chip. "Say, Coach, wouldn't a zone defense have stopped Parkton?"

"We'd have used a zone if necessary, Chip, but I'd rather hold up our special defenses until we really need them. Don't forget, it wasn't our defense that whipped us at Parkton—it was our offense."

"Boy, I sure feel better today than I did on Thursday!" Chet Stewart breathed a relieved sigh.

"I guess we all do," Coach Rockwell agreed. "Can you imagine how we would have felt coming back to Valley Falls if we'd lost all three games?"

"They'd probably have run us out of town!" Chet laughed.

"Probably will anyway." Coach Rockwell smiled. "They're hard to please!"

Valley Falls was hoops crazy! The Big Reds were on fire. Following the Salem game, Valley Falls walked all over Steeltown, Hampton, Dulane, and Northville. The victories over Hampton, Dulane, and Northville were expected, but no one except Soapy Smith had figured the Big Reds to take Steeltown. Today they were leaving on the second road trip of the season, the one that would have a great deal to do with their chances for sectional honors.

It seemed as if the whole town, in holiday mood, was at the school. Students and residents from all over town were holding an impromptu pep rally, and crowds surrounded the team bus while pictures were taken. People were yelling, cheering, and giving the team a real send-off this time. Past mistakes and disappointments were forgotten. The town and the school were proud of its team. Everybody loved a winner!

The bus was a beauty, decorated in red and white with pennants flying and with "Special" spelled out in the front. Special it was!

This trip might well be one to remember; the team record was now eight victories, nine counting the alumni game, and only two defeats. Everyone was talking about the Big Reds and the state championship. Could be, too, Chip thought, if the Big Reds could win on the road!

Everyone was waving and hollering, "Bring back the victories!"

"Keep punching, guys!"

"Look out for those Cardinals!"

"We'll be watching you!"

"Don't let Soapy jump out!"

Then the bus was moving; the team let out a great cheer, and the players were on their way again. Soapy bounced up and down in his seat, yelling, "Here we go again, guys. And this time we're really rollin'!"

The arrival at Cary seemed almost a repeat of departure from Valley Falls. Tech's big band at the hotel was brassy and loud, and the crowd cheered the Big Reds again and again.

"You'd think we were state champs," said Speed.

"Could be, pal! Could be," said Red.

"Could be, nothing," broke in Soapy. "We is, pal. We *is!*"

The team piled out of the bus and gathered in front of the desk in the hotel lobby. Chip had the room keys, but before passing them out, he got everyone's attention and read Coach Rockwell's schedule.

"Lunch at one o'clock. Team strategy at two-thirty. Everyone in bed from three until four-thirty. Pregame snack—five o'clock. Five-thirty, ten-minute walk. Five-forty-five, back to bed. Seven o'clock we meet in the lobby and go out and beat Tech!"

Everyone cheered. Spirits were high!

Looking up from the *Sports Illustrated* basketball article, Chip glanced across the room toward the bed from which faint snores started and drifted through the room. "What a guy!" he laughed to himself. "In bed and already sound asleep at this hour."

He looked at his watch. It was just ten o'clock. He again immersed himself in the McCallum article. A little later, finished reading, he glanced again at Taps—dead to the world. Chip was a little tired too. He leaned back in the chair.

What a trip this had been! Soapy was right. The Big Reds were rolling—rolling up the scores too! They'd been right at home on Tech's big court and had walked away with the game, 55-40. Stratford had been tough—for three quarters. Then Speed and Red had gone to work with their give-and-go plays. Speed scored sixteen points, and Red got fourteen; their total was almost more than that of the whole Stratford team. Valley Falls 50, Stratford 32.

Chip breathed a sigh of satisfaction. Two down and only Weston to go. Yes, only the Cardinals. But the

Cardinals would be really tough at home. They hadn't forgotten that first defeat in two years; they'd definitely be looking for this chance to even up with the Big Reds the next night.

Everything was going well. No, not everything. Chip hadn't completely forgotten the money box, that three-week mystery still remained unsolved. Coach Rockwell had kept him so busy lately, he'd hardly had time to think. Who had been in that crowd by the table? Chip struggled to form a mental picture of the memory . . . Harry Nichols and Ted Williams . . . Joe Kennedy of the *Times* . . . Pete Williams of the *Post* . . . Wheels Ferris . . . and Fats Ohlsen!

He jumped as the telephone shrilled. It was Chet Stewart.

"Chip?"

"Yes, Coach."

"Check all the rooms. See that everyone's in and report back."

"Sure, Coach, right away."

Chip hurried along the halls, knocking on the doors of the rooms he had listed. "Open up, you guys. Get to bed! Get some sleep!"

"OK, Chip!"

"Got to win that game tomorrow."

"It's a snap—it'll be a piece of cake, Chipper," called Speed as Chip hurried down the hall.

The players always doubled up on the trips. Chip and Taps usually roomed together. At Room 1214 he got no answer. He checked the list; yes, the room number was correct. It was the room Rock had assigned to Mike Rodriguez and Lefty Peters. He knocked several times, but still there was no answer. What was the matter? He went back to his room and called Room 1214. Still no answer.

Stewart had said to report right back. He was probably waiting right now for the call. What to do? What *could* he do? What could he tell Coach Stewart?

It was ten minutes after eleven by his watch. He'd try the lobby. No luck! He'd call once more and check the hotel register. No, his room list was correct. Now he had to report to Stewart.

"Come in, Chip. All check?"

"Went to every room, Coach."

"That's good. Thanks, Chipper. You'd better get some sleep yourself. See you in the morning."

Outside the door Chip paused. "There I go again," he muttered. "If Coach Rockwell finds out about this, he'll never trust me again. Why do I think he trusts me now?"

Chip's thoughts turned again to the missing money box. He knows I'm responsible; so does the whole school. I've just got to get that box back.

Fats had been right beside it. He *could* be the one; he needed the money to pay those men and get his phony checks back. He *must* have taken it! *I'm just going to have to go see J. P. Ohlsen . . . and I don't mean Joel Palmer Ohlsen Jr.*

Back in his room Chip called Mike and Lefty's room again. Still no answer! What could have happened to those two? What a spot to be in.

Next morning Chip hurried down to Room 1214 and banged on the door. Mike Rodriguez greeted him cheerfully. Chip wasted no time.

"Where'd you guys go last night?" he challenged, looking from one player to the other.

"Movies. Why?" asked Mike nonchalantly.

"Why?" demanded Chip angrily. "Why? Because everyone was supposed to be in bed by eleven. That's why!"

"We lost track of the time, Chip. The movie got out late," Lefty apologized lamely.

"You knew the show would be late, and you knew you were supposed to be in too! What's the matter with you anyway?" Chip glared at him and then snapped, "You know how Rock is about things like that!"

"Does he know we weren't in?" Mike asked, alarmed.

"No, he doesn't! Chet asked me to check and report, but I didn't tell him."

"Thanks, Chip."

"Don't thank me! I don't want any thanks for that! I had to let Coach Stewart down just because you didn't care enough to get in on time. Especially the night before the most important game on the schedule."

"Sorry, Chip, it won't happen again."

Chip slammed the door and joined the crowd in the lobby.

Coach Rockwell and Chet Stewart were seated in one corner, talking quietly.

"What time did you say they got in, Coach?" Stewart was puzzled.

"I saw them about a quarter to twelve. Just the two of them."

"Do you think they had just gone out?"

"No," said Coach Rockwell, "I think they were just coming in. Probably been to a movie."

"Did they see you?"

"Don't think so. They were pretty much in a hurry."

"Wonder why Chip didn't tell me?"

"Did you expect him to, Chet?" Rockwell regarded Stewart quizzically. "You made a mistake there, Chet. Never ask a kid to check up on his teammates. It isn't fair!" His voice was just a bit sharp as he concluded, "Forget the whole thing! I don't go for tattletales!"

CHAMPIONSHIP BALL

What a team! Everybody in Valley Falls was patting the players on the back and talking about the tournament. Hadn't the Big Reds beaten Weston again? And on Weston's own floor? This squad was the first team to beat the Cardinals on their own floor in seven years! It took the Rock and Valley Falls to do the unexpected. Hadn't they won all three road games on this trip and two out of three on the first one? That was playing ball!

Wait until the tournament! Section Two was just as good as wrapped up. What if the Big Reds were tied with Weston at eleven victories and two defeats. Hadn't they given Weston those two defeats? Sure, they had! What was more, the last game at Weston had been decisive. They'd beaten the Cardinals 53-41. The Big Reds were back in the fight for state honors. There was a little bit of swagger when the fans talked about the Big Reds now. The players swaggered a bit too.

But two interested people weren't swaggering: Coach Rockwell and Chet Stewart. The two coaches were seated in the athletic office. Stewart was looking out the window, his eyes focused on the big stadium in back of the gym. Coach Rockwell was sitting behind his desk, fingering a sheaf of newspaper clippings.

Stewart broke the silence. "They're pretty cocky, Coach! They're pretty cocky!"

"I know, Chet. I know they are. Most kids would feel pretty good if they read all this ink about them." He shoved the sports articles aside.

"What are you gonna do about it?" Chet worried.

"Nothing right now, I guess. Sometimes a team needs a lot of confidence. Sometimes it helps!"

"Yeah, but this is the wrong kind of confidence, Coach. They think they're world-beaters!" Chet was disgusted.

"Who do they think they are? Why don't you knock them down a bit? That's what you used to do to us," he said hopefully.

"Maybe so, Chet, but there isn't much rhyme or reason trying to compare boys of today with kids of your time and mine. Everything changes."

"Everything but you, Coach." Chet laughed. "You'll never change!"

CHAPTER 18

Turning Points

SOUTHERN'S TEAM was made up of five kids who had played together all through grade school. They had entered high school as a group and had made headlines as Southern's reserve team. Now the varsity, they played like champions. Their team play was perfect, and time and time again they dashed down the floor to score easy points with their quick breakaway attack. Rodriguez and Peters were caught out of position again and again.

Chip, at the scorer's table, was squirming, pushing, elbowing, and making every play. Why didn't Coach do something? What was wrong with Speed? Why didn't he call for a time-out?

Just then, as if by mental telepathy, Speed called, "Time!"

Chip looked at the scoreboard and the clock. Southern 40. Valley Falls 22. Eighteen points behind. It just couldn't be done.

TURNING POINTS

Coach Rockwell substituted Soapy Smith for Lefty Peters. Soapy, all excited and sputtering, rushed up to Speed. "Coach said to go into a zone right away!"

"A zone?" Speed was bewildered. "A zone when we're eighteen points behind? Are you sure, Soapy?"

"That's what he said!"

"OK. Zone it is! But one of us is crazy! Now look, guys—"

For the next six minutes Chip was kept so busy marking baskets, fouls, and free throws that he never even knew the score.

"Hello, folks—this is Stan Gomez—WTKO takes you now to the Valley Falls-Southern High basketball game at Valley Falls. And, believe you me, we're catching the climax of a hectic game. After trailing 40-22 midway through the third quarter, Valley Falls has climbed back into this game! The score now: Southern 44, Valley Falls 40! Two minutes to play.

"Valley Falls's Morris and Schwartz are playing the game of their lives, and Taps Browning, the kid who has been handicapped with a bad ankle all year, seems to have finally found himself. Speed Morris and Red Schwartz are fighting like madmen under both baskets. Browning is scoring with turn-around jump shots reminiscent of Chip Hilton.

"There he goes—up again—and it's *in*! The score now is 44-42, Southern leading. Minute and a half to play. Southern has the ball out of bounds now—in to Glasco—he's dribbling down the middle of the court—he passes to Southern's big center, Ford—there's a foul! No—it's not on Valley Falls—it's on Ford. After Ford received the ball, he turned and shoved Browning with his elbow. That's the seventh team foul, and Browning goes to the line.

"Browning is on the free-throw line now. He has a chance to close the gap on this shot—score is 44-42. Browning shoots—it's *good!* Score now, 44-43. Fifty seconds to play. The second one is good too! We're tied at 44 for each squad.

"It's Southern's ball out of bounds again. They're bringing the ball up the court—they're trying to hold it— Valley Falls is waiting—Southern is passing to Glasco— back to Ford—over to Kimmel. The ball is in the front-court now—Valley Falls is gradually pressing Southern back toward the ten-second line.

"Hold it! There's a foul! Looks as if it's against Valley Falls—it is! Coach Whitcomb is on his feet. He's waving instructions to Glasco. Yep! Glasco is on the line. He shoots and—he misses. Listen to that crowd!

"Taps Browning takes the rebound—he passes over to Schwartz. Schwartz is dribbling down the floor— Morris has the ball now, in the corner. Back to Schwartz—it goes over to Peters—to Rodriguez. Rodriguez dribbles in and—there's a foul on Ford again. Ford switched to stop Rodriguez and fouled him just before the shot. Valley Falls has a chance to win this game now.

"Rodriguez is on the line. He's one of the best shots in the state. The referee hands the ball to Rodriguez— Rodriguez checks out the clock—only seconds to play now—he bounces the ball three times at the free-throw line—he shoots! It's GOOD! The second shot rings the hoop as Ford of Southern snares the rebound.

"Southern's ball now, five seconds to play. There's a long pass—it's intercepted—Morris leaped high in the air to grab that ball. There's the horn—the game's over! Valley Falls wins, 45-44. What a game!"

Valley Falls fans couldn't believe it, and Chip, sitting at the scorer's table, wouldn't believe it. *Lose* to Dane? It was impossible! Why the Danes hadn't won more than four games all year. Everyone had beaten them—that is, up until February when Myers, the big transfer center from Cortley, had joined the team.

Dane had taken the lead at the very start of the game and had never been less than ten points ahead. Now in the last quarter, Valley Falls was fourteen points behind—and getting nowhere fast.

The Big Reds just couldn't get going. The Scott twins were fighting their heads off, but they made too many mistakes—bad passes, traveled with the ball, didn't pick up quick enough on the defense, didn't switch—

Chip was conscious of someone talking, expressing his thoughts. It was his own voice. He was talking out loud. Things must be bad! "Why, even without Rodriguez and Lefty we ought to beat Dane! They don't have a thing except Myers, and Taps is playing him better than even—"

Chip quickly checked the scorebook. Anxiously scanning the totals, he was relieved to see the book was all in Taps's favor. Taps had scored thirteen points and Myers had seven, so far. Points weren't everything, but Taps was passing off well on the pivot, and he was getting his share of the rebounds. If Myers outplayed Taps, Jerry Davis and all the fans would be all over Coach Rockwell's case for not letting Myers transfer to play for Valley Falls. If only Mike and Lefty were in there . . .

Speed and Red were battling furiously. Time and again Speed drove in—trying to pull the game out single-handedly. The Dane guards couldn't hold him, yet there was so little time left to play. With five minutes to go, Soapy Smith was substituted for Matt Scott. Soapy played like a tiger. He was in every play—fighting, talking, encouraging his teammates.

The Dane player guarding Soapy floated away to help double-team Morris. Speed rifled the ball to Soapy, who electrified everyone by dropping in a long jumper from the side; minutes later, he did it again, and then again—aiming the ball each time as if his life depended upon it. His last goal cut the Dane lead to six points.

Chip was cheering every play, pounding the table and elbowing the Dane scorer seated next to him on each movement of the ball. Speed scored again, and then Soapy dropped in another set. Chip looked at the time.

Now only one minute was left to play—two points behind . . . forty seconds . . . thirty seconds . . . twenty! The whistle! A foul!

Chip groaned and buried his head in his hands. Oh, no! . . . it's on Speed . . . that's the end! He glanced up just as the second free throw dropped cleanly through the hoop. Four points behind. Before Valley Falls even had a chance to try another shot, the buzzer ended the game. The final score: Dane 50, Valley Falls 46.

A quiet crowd of fans filed out of the gym and down the steps to the street. Usually the whole neighborhood rang with laughter, shouts, and cheers. Tonight everyone seemed in a hurry. The fans were down. Way down!

Ironically, earlier that very evening, Stan Gomez had "shot the stars" for Valley Falls. The fans had all listened. Gomez had rated the Big Reds the best team in Section Two—probably the best in the state. Now, not three hours later, those stars had all blinked out in thin air. Valley Falls had lost to the weakest team on its schedule. And on the home court!

"Delford and Salem are next. If we couldn't beat Dane, how can we beat those two? There goes the tournament!"

"Lefty Peters beat Weston almost by himself, and Rockwell didn't use him at all tonight. Why, come to think of it, Peters wasn't even dressed!"

"That Dane team doesn't have a thing. If Mike Rodriguez had been in there, we would have beaten them by fifteen points!"

"I hear there's dissension on the team. Too many stars! Too much publicity!"

"What are you talking about? Why, Browning musta got twice as many points as Myers. Played him to a standstill. Myers didn't beat us—it was those Scott kids; they've had no experience."

"Been readin' their clippin's! Got swelled heads!"

"Rock dropped Rodriguez and Peters just tonight. Broke training, they say."

"Rockwell's too tough! He still coaches like the old days. He's got to get in touch with today's kids. Players in this generation are different—he's got to give them more slack—loosen up a little. First, he dropped Sanders, and now he's canned Rodriguez and Peters. Just when we looked like a sure thing for the state. Doesn't he know it's winning that counts?"

Chip, Speed, and Taps sat silently in Speed's Mustang. The row of parked cars had departed long before; yet Speed made no move to start his engine. There was no need to rush down to the Sugar Bowl.

Chip's thoughts turned to Coach Rockwell. Bet he wasn't drawing pictures or writing names this evening.

Some of Coach Rockwell's pet philosophies and sayings ran through his mind.

"On the sports pages you're a hero today and the forgotten man tomorrow!"

"Success is not measured by the number of lines of publicity you get but by the way you play the game."

"Some of you fellows have been chasing headlines. The quicker you stop reading the sports columns and start to play basketball, the quicker we'll get back in the winning column."

"There are turning points in every game. Some people call those the breaks of the game. They're not breaks. Those turning points are the result of constant concentration by intelligent players. Some players have the ability to concentrate at all times—winning or losing— other players concentrate only when it means the plaudits of the crowd. The *real* athlete concentrates all the way—permits nothing except the game to enter his mind. That's why *he's* a champion."

Chip's thoughts moved into other channels. Ever since the first road trip, he had been trying to decide what he should do about the money box and his suspicions about Joel Ohlsen. During the month since the theft of the Weston gate receipts, the speculation and talk at Valley Falls High School had died down somewhat. The disappearance was no longer mentioned in the *Yellow Jacket,* but Chip could not forget what had happened.

No matter how hard he tried to keep his mind off the box, the incident came popping back up—and Joel Ohlsen with it!

Telling J. P. about Joel's gambling debt and his suspicions regarding the box seemed like a dirty thing to do, but

TURNING POINTS

something *had* to be done. That box was his responsibility, and he was not going to fool around any longer.

Right after his football injury, J. P. Ohlsen had said he could always come to him at any time for advice or help. Well, it was time. This was going to hurt: this was difficult.

He considered the possibility of confronting Fats directly. No, he wouldn't get anywhere that way. Fats would just laugh at him. Well, J.P. wouldn't laugh. Chip would get action there, of one kind or another.

Speed broke the silence. "What are we going to do about Mike and Lefty?"

"We've sure got to do something," Chip replied absent-mindedly.

"I don't think Coach will let 'em play anymore this year," said Taps. His long legs filled the back seat of the car, and his arms, hanging loosely, nearly reached the floor. He was entirely oblivious to the cold; in fact, he even had the window open.

"Someone ought to ask the coach to give 'em another chance," said Speed.

"Stop sidestepping the real issue," said Chip. "You know the only question left is which one of us is going to talk to the coach. Who's it going to be, the captain or the manager?" Chip proceeded slowly and added quietly, "I think it should be the captain, Speed."

"What? Think I'm crazy?"

"Seems to me it's your responsibility. You're the captain."

"I know. But come on, Chip. You know I can't talk to Rock like you can. No one can!"

Chip sat quietly for a few minutes. No one said anything. Then he elbowed Speed. "OK, I'll talk to him. I've got to see somebody else too. I might as well have a showdown *all* around!"

CHAPTER 19

Real Courage

JOEL OHLSEN'S collar on his polo shirt was drenched and so was his spirit when he walked out of Coach Rockwell's office. He had just passed through the worst hour of his life. His ears were burning, and his face was fiery red. Although he should have felt happier than he had ever dreamed possible, his heart remained heavy. His tightly clasped hand held three pieces of paper—three pink checks totaling nearly a thousand dollars!

Ohlsen was filled with mixed emotions: a sense of relief from the pressure that had been eating at him since the night of his gambling, a feeling of shame because of his actions and the stern lecture Coach Rockwell had just given him, and a glow of gratitude because his conscience had found rest. Yes, Coach Rockwell had poured it on, but he felt grateful even for that.

Wheels was waiting for him. "What happened?" he asked breathlessly.

"What happened?" echoed Joel. "Look!" He held out the checks. "That's what happened. What a guy! What a guy!"

"The coach?"

"Sure! Nobody else! I've had him wrong all along." He regarded Wheels thoughtfully. "Guess I've had a lot of things wrong." Joel stopped abruptly. His eyes were puzzled. "Wheels," he began, "you know something really strange?"

"What?"

"Rockwell told me Chip Hilton and Biggie Cohen got him to go down to Mike's and get those checks. I can't understand it! Of all people!"

"Hilton and Cohen?"

"Yeah, Hilton and Cohen. I don't get it!"

"I told you all along they were OK guys, Joel."

"I know, Wheels, but right or wrong, those guys ought to hate me. Wonder what made them do a thing like that for me?" Ohlsen was completely confused. "And how did they even find out about it?" he pondered aloud.

Wheels didn't answer. Wheels wouldn't answer. He was thinking about Biggie Cohen. Biggie hadn't let him down; Joel didn't know . . .

A serious Joel Ohlsen interrupted their silence. "Coach said the gamblers had given the checks back on their own and the debt was canceled. Said the whole thing was probably part of a plot to teach me a lesson. Wonder if he was kiddin' me?" He paused. "What a clueless fool I've been!"

Wheels nodded his head. "You were that, all right," he said. "I'm glad now my father kept *me* out of that joint."

"Coach made me promise to stay away from there, too, Wheels. And you know what?"

"What?"

"I'm *gonna* do it! You know what else I'm gonna do?"

"What?"

"I'm gonna go see Biggie and Chip and apologize."

"They'll probably drop dead from the shock of it all!" Wheels exclaimed and then laughed.

"It'll probably kill me too. I never apologized to anyone before in my life. But, Coach said humbling ourselves is not a sign of weakness. He said admitting we're wrong takes courage. I sure owe those two guys a lot. Makes me feel pretty cheap. Especially after the trick I pulled on Chip Hilton."

"What trick?"

Ohlsen took a deep breath. "You remember the night we beat Weston?"

"Yeah."

"Hear anything about someone stealin' the gate receipts from Hilton that night?"

"Sure! Why?"

"Well—*I'm* the guy."

"You mean—*you* took the box? How? When? What'd ya do with it?"

"Remember when we stopped in the hall after the game, and Hilton was showing everyone the scorebook? Well, I saw the box on the table, and, well, for some reason, I just dropped my coat over it and—well, you know the rest."

"What did you do with it?"

"Still got it! Box and all! I've been tryin' to figure out a way to get it back—that is, till this afternoon. First, I figured I'd use the money to get back the checks, but something held me back. Just couldn't do it. Now I'm sure glad I didn't touch any of the money."

REAL COURAGE

Wheels's mouth fell open. "What are you gonna do with it?"

Ohlsen didn't answer. He was deep in thought.

"Give it to me, Joel," Wheels whispered. "I'll get it back! I'll slip it up on Rockwell's porch and ring the doorbell and run."

"It's too late for that, Wheels. I told the coach all about it—I'm supposed to take the box over to his house tonight."

"As I live and breathe!" Wheels gasped.

They stood in silence, each boy busy with his own thoughts. Joel suddenly squared his shoulders and muttered, "I've got to do it myself! Just got to!"

"Do what?" Wheels asked as Ohlsen started up the hill.

"Tell Joel Palmer Ohlsen Sr. a mystery story," Fats answered.

All the way home, Wheels was puzzled by Joel's cryptic remark. As he passed the side door leading into Sorelli's, he stopped his thoughts long enough to throw a loud Bronx cheer in the direction of Mike Sorelli's business.

Although it was bitter cold, Chip Hilton was starting to perspire as he stood in the phone booth.

"But it's a personal matter, Mr. Ohlsen. It's about Joel, and I'd rather see you at your house. It's awfully important. You told me last fall in the hospital to call on you anytime . . . I have to work tonight, sir. I'd rather get it over with this afternoon, right away. . . . It is important! That's right, it's about Joel, sir. Yes, sir. All right, sir. I'll be there in fifteen minutes!"

Chip trudged up the winding driveway leading to the big Ohlsen house. Not many years back, he and Joel had spent many happy hours on these grounds and playing together at this house. But that was before Chip's father's death, before the bullying by Joel had destroyed their grade school friendship.

In those days he had always dashed straight up the big wide steps three at a time, yelling to Joel, "Hurry up!"

Today he had taken the long way—postponing a little longer his upcoming interview with J. P. Ohlsen. The closer his dragging footsteps brought him to the big house, the lower his heart sank. J. P.'s big Cadillac was parked in the side drive as Chip went up the porch steps one at a time.

In the library, waiting with a tight chest and a thumping heart, he tried to collect his thoughts and plan his words, but his mind just wouldn't function. He prayed for the right words to deliver the difficult message. For a brief moment, he was tempted to cut and run—to make some excuse and leave well enough alone.

"Hello, Chip. I hope there's nothing wrong at home. Sit down." J. P. smiled warmly and motioned Chip to a chair.

Too late now. Well, here goes. . . .

"Thank you, sir. No, sir. Everything's all right at home." Chip gulped, and then he plunged.

"Mr. Ohlsen, when I was in the hospital, you said I could always come to you for help at any time."

"That's right, Chip. What's this all about?"

"Fats, I mean Joel, sir. It's about Joel and the money box."

"Money box? What money box?"

"The money box that was stolen—I mean that disappeared—the night of the Weston game."

"How does that concern Joel or me, Chip?"

"Well, I—I think Joel took it!" Chip held his breath.

"What's that? What did you say? What do you mean?"

"I think Joel took the box, Mr. Ohlsen."

J. P. Ohlsen straightened up in his chair and regarded Hilton with amazement. "What on earth are you talking about? What would Joel want with the box?"

"He needed money, sir. He needed money badly."

"Joel *needed* money? What for?"

Chip was silent. Finally, under J. P. Ohlsen's stern gaze, he said, "I'd rather not say, sir." Then he added firmly, "But I *know* he took the box!"

"Why, Chip, I've never heard anything so preposterous in all my life! That is a very serious accusation, Hilton."

"I know, but—"

In the hall outside the library, Joel Ohlsen stood listening intently to the conversation in the book-lined room. Under one arm he clutched the black money box. He breathed deeply and stepped into the room.

"Dad, what Chip says is true!"

J. P. turned and stared incredulously at his son. His eyes shifted to the box and back again to Joel's face. He shook his head slowly in bewilderment.

"I—I don't understand," he said, sinking back in his chair and regarding Joel blankly.

"Everything Chip said is true!" Joel stated flatly. "I *did* need money, and I *did* take the box! But, I didn't use the money. It's all still here. I told Coach Rockwell all about it just a little while ago." He faced his father with a set face and steady eyes.

Chip rose to his feet and nervously bit his lips. "I'm— I'm sorry, Joel," he managed. "Honest."

Joel's determined face softened as he turned to Chip.

"I'm the one who's sorry, Chip—" His voice broke and he sank into a chair, covering his face with his hands.

J. P. Ohlsen rose from his chair, pressed a trembling hand to his forehead, and moved slowly to the window.

Chip stopped beside Joel just long enough to grip the shaking shoulder. "It's OK, Joel. Everything'll come out all right."

Chip again chose the winding driveway instead of the long flight of steps. From the library window, with empty eyes J. P. Ohlsen watched the dragging steps of the boy who had just brought the worst news ever to enter the big home's front door.

Long after Hilton had passed from view, J. P. stood in the window, reliving the past few minutes and the years they represented. His thoughts ranged from this house to the big pottery and back again. The ultimate goal of all the years he had devoted to building up the Valley Falls Pottery to its present position had been to leave his son a proud heritage.

But he had forgotten the most important thing; he had forgotten those important years when his son needed him most, needed something more than a car, a weekly allowance, and an indulgent mother.

A growing boy needed the guidance and understanding of a man, but he'd been too busy. Well, he'd *have* to take a hand now. In the past when he had tried to interfere with Mrs. Ohlsen's pampering of Joel, his efforts had always led to a family quarrel, a quarrel that ended with Joel's mother in tears and Joel in sullen silence.

Joel had shown *real* courage this afternoon. Maybe it wasn't too late. With a change of atmosphere and a curtailment of such luxuries as a car and too much leisure time . . . maybe a little closer supervision . . . tighter reins, then perhaps the boy's reactions would determine whether he was made of the right stuff!

"Not all the clay that has to be molded is at my pottery," J. P. thought as he turned to comfort his son.

CHAPTER 20

The Score That Counts

AS THE seven o'clock sportscast ended, Speed Morris reached up and snapped off the TV. "Wonder what's keepin' him?" he asked, glancing around the room at the somber faces. There was no reply. Each boy was busy with his own thoughts.

Practice that afternoon had been terrible. Everyone had expected a real going-over from the coach, but he had said nothing about the Dane game. Chet Stewart had run the squad through warm-ups and several passing and dribbling drills, and then Coach Rockwell had unveiled a new offensive formation. But something was missing. The pep and excitement, the exuberance and spontaneous yelling, the good-natured kidding—all were gone! It was a defeated squad!

After a short, slow-motion workout, Coach Rockwell had dismissed the team with a weary "That's all, boys."

In the locker room, Speed had gone from player to player, talking in a lowered voice. Later, he had looked up Mike and Lefty, and now all the guys were gathered in the big family room of the Hilton home.

Chip wasn't there. According to the plan, he was to see Coach Rockwell right after practice with a sincere plea from the squad for Mike and Lefty.

It was nearly nine o'clock before they heard Hilton's dragging steps. Even before he entered the room, the worried group of boys knew the answer. All eyes were on Chip as he dropped wearily on the couch.

"No improvement, guys," he said.

"You mean we're through for the season?" Lefty's voice was shaky.

"Looks that way."

"Must have been a tough session," ventured Taps.

"No, just the opposite, Taps. Coach was fine. Said he appreciated how we all felt, but there was nothing he could or would do about it. Said Mike and Lefty knew the rules same as Pat Sanders did, and they'd have to take the consequences—which they also knew."

"Seems to me it's more like penalizing the team!" said Ryan Scott.

"Seems the same to me!" echoed Matt.

There was a long silence. Mike pressed his lips tightly together as he gazed dejectedly at Chip, and Lefty Peters hunched over looking steadily at the floor. Every boy in the room was thinking the same thing—*There goes the tournament!*

Red Schwartz was bitter. "What in the world was he snoopin' around Mike Sorelli's for anyway?"

Chip could have told Schwartz a lot about *that*. The Rock must have gone down there again to pick up

THE SCORE THAT COUNTS

Fats's checks. It seemed as if Fats Ohlsen spelled trouble in more ways than one. If he hadn't gambled, there wouldn't have been any bad checks . . . no missing box . . . no session with J. P. like the one this afternoon . . . no need for Coach Rockwell to go to Sorelli's. And then Lefty and Mike would still be on the team.

"It was my fault!" Lefty's voice was filled with self-disgust. "We were on our way home, and I thought there wouldn't be any harm in watching them shoot a little while. Mike didn't want to go. We never dreamed we'd run into him."

"How come Sorelli let you in?" asked Schwartz. "He's been running all the high school guys out lately."

"He didn't see us—we went in the side door."

"I never dreamed it was so late," said Mike.

"What time was it?" someone asked.

"Must have been after 11:30."

"No wonder the Rock was upset!" Soapy moaned. "Well, there's no use sittin' here with our chins on the floor. We ain't gonna give up. We gotta do something!"

"Soapy's got the right idea," said Chip. "We've got to win those next two games."

"Won't do us any good if we do win!" Red growled. "We're already out of the running—with three losses. Steeltown's only got one more game—Southern. They'll murder them!"

"Don't be too sure about that," said Chip. "Don't forget Southern gave us real tough competition, and we had Mike and Lefty playin' too. They might do it!"

"Southern will beat Steeltown!" Soapy looked challengingly at Schwartz. "I can feel it!"

"It won't make any difference unless we beat D 'ford and Salem," said Chip. "Let's concentrate on them. What d'ya say?"

"The Scotts can do it!" said Mike. "They're just as good as Lefty and me."

"They'll have to do it," nodded Chip. "Say, Speed, you know what I think?" Without waiting for a reply he continued, "I think if we all worked with Ryan and Matt and went over all of Coach's stuff every night after practice, we'd be hard to beat. Ryan and Matt just don't know it well enough, that's all. Maybe we could all pitch in and teach it to 'em. What do you think?"

"Sounds good." Speed assented. "We could move back everything here in the room and walk through the stuff. We'll have to. We play Delford in four days."

"That's enough time if you guys get together here every night and go over and over it," said Chip. He looked around the circle of faces. "Well, how about it?"

Bill English had been quiet all evening, but he voiced everyone's feelings when he said, "Look, the whole town's counting us out. Everyone but the Rock—he never gives up on us! We won't quit either! Let's win those next two games if we have to practice all night!"

"That's it—it's settled!" Speed jumped to his feet, holding out his two hands. "Well, what's it going to be, guys?"

Everyone in the room rushed to form the circle and join hands with his teammates. "We'll do it!"

The next morning Coach Rockwell was sitting stiffly behind his desk. His black eyes were focused steadily on Rogers's face.

"After all," Rogers was saying, "it's a police matter! You just can't do things like that when it's a police affair, Hank."

"We've got the money back! No harm's been done."

"It isn't a question of whether harm has been done or not. You know that as well as I do. But the police have been investigating the matter for the past month. You'll never get away with it!"

"I'm not trying to get away with anything."

"Maybe not, but you're putting yourself in a position where you're sort of an accessory after the fact. Have you thought about that?"

"Yes, I have."

"OK, it's your funeral."

"There'll be no funeral. You know, Rogers, this might be just as good a time as any for you and me to get squared away." Coach Rockwell's voice hardened, and his eyes narrowed dangerously.

"You and I have been dancing around the bigger issue long enough. It's time you knew my philosophy about this teaching and coaching game. Teaching and coaching aren't just mediums for turning out mental wizards and athletic champions. They're something bigger that goes on here. It's what you put into the heart and soul of a kid that counts. Not when he's on top and everything's OK, but when he needs help. Everyone's made mistakes; you've made them, and I've made them.

"Teaching and coaching give people like you and me a chance to do more for a kid than his own parents! Kids can really talk to us—and they do! They also depend on us and need us. That's right where you and I differ; you don't believe a teacher or the coach should get mixed up in a kid's personal or family problems. Well, that's your business. I happen to feel the other way about it!

"Joel Ohlsen made a mistake. He needed help, and I gave it to him—with *no* reservations. I told him I'd take care of his gambling checks and the money box problem—*and I mean to do it!*

CHAMPIONSHIP BALL

"Joel Ohlsen is the son of one of the most influential men in town; he could engineer your discharge and mine. But, as a father, well, as a father he's a good provider. But that isn't enough. You know it, and so do I! Joel Ohlsen has made a bad mistake, and he's got to be punished. But there are other ways to punish a kid besides throwing him in jail and putting a mark on him for life. That kid didn't have to tell me about taking that box— but he *did*! What's more, he told his *father* too. We both know J. P. Ohlsen well enough to know he'll take care of the punishment end of it.

"I got my first insight into Joel Ohlsen's character when I had to throw him off the football squad. He showed me then what too much money and too much personal freedom can do to a teenage boy's character. Joel probably has hated me ever since the football incident too. But I know that Joel Ohlsen and I got closer together yesterday afternoon than he's ever been with his father.

"Most kids idealize and idolize anyone who's active in sports. It's educators like you and me—people who know the real score and who talk the kid's language—that a kid needs and turns to when he's in trouble.

"Well, I'm not going to let that kid down! You handle the business end of the athletics; *I'll* keep score of the kids!"

CHAPTER 21

Down the Stretch

THE USUAL locker room banter and needling were missing. Pop and Chet looked at each other with puzzled eyes as they surveyed the resolute, determined faces of the Big Reds. Little by little, the same spirit engulfed Chet and Pop; they worked quickly and quietly, strapping ankles and checking equipment.

Chip held his breath as he handed the scorebook to Rockwell. What if Rock didn't start Matt and Ryan? All their plans would go out the window!

He watched Rock pencil in names: Morris, Schwartz, Browning. Rockwell hesitated and looked around the room. His eyes concentrated on the Scott twins for a second and then he quickly wrote down M. Scott and R. Scott.

Chip breathed a sigh of relief and caught Speed's eye. A grim smile passed between them—so far so good. A slap on the back turned his attention to the coach. Coach Rockwell regarded him with a quizzical smile. "OK?" he asked.

"What's that, Coach? I—I don't understand, Coach," Chip stammered.

"Isn't that what you've been holding secret practices for—over at the Hilton A.C.?"

Chip was stumped for words. How did he do it? Rock seemed to know everything.

Coach Jenkins had his boys in a huddle in front of their bench. Delford's center, Red Henry, towered above the group. Jenkins accentuated each word as he struck the palm of his left hand with a clenched right fist. "If you never win another game in your life, win this one! Let's knock them right out of the tournament! Tonight!"

The Delford-Valley Falls games always produced bitter competition, regardless of the quality of the teams. This game was more like a grudge fight between Jenkins and Rockwell. There was none of the usual handshaking and friendly good-luck expressions before the game— merely a cool "Hi ya, Rock," and a "Hello, Jenkins." The game was on.

Taps got a clean tip to Red Schwartz, and before the game clock had ticked off ten seconds, Valley Falls scored on a brilliant turn-around jump shot by Speed. A fighting Big Reds team faced Delford. Delford didn't have a chance—the first half was no contest. The Big Reds were pouring it on with a vengeance. What a reversal of play for the team! Matt and Ryan Scott passed carefully and played the game just the way Coach Rockwell had drilled Mike Rodriguez and Lefty Peters. Rockwell was amazed at their cool play; they were never out of position on the court, and their defense was unwavering.

Speed and Red discarded their famous give-and-go plays and were cutting around Taps on play after play. Taps would maneuver under the basket until Speed and Red were all set—then he would break out to meet the ball. Speed and Red would "split the post" or drive their opponents into Taps and then cut toward the basket for a return pass and an open shot.

Red Henry, the big Delford center, was good, but he had never been challenged to switch with every play. When Speed or Red cut behind or in front of Taps, Henry had to switch or let them take an unguarded shot. Before the end of the second quarter, he carried four personal fouls against him. Speed and Red were too fast, and he had been forced to foul them as they drove to the basket.

The fans had completely forgotten the upset by Dane; they cheered the Big Reds to the rafters. This was basketball as it should be played! At the half, Valley Falls led 31-20. Coach Jenkins had scouted the Big Reds thoroughly, but he was caught flat-footed. He had prepared a defense for the give-and-go specialties of Speed and Red and for Browning's under-the-basket shots but had mapped no defense for Coach Rockwell's new offense.

Between the halves, the Valley Falls fans began to feel as they had after the triumphant road trip:

"Rock is at it again!"

"You can't keep the old boy down!"

"Sure knows how to use his players."

"You can see he's been working on those Scott kids— what a difference since the last game!"

"Too bad they didn't play like that last week!"

But Coach Jenkins changed his defense for the second half. When Speed threw the first ball in to Taps, all five Delford players floated back between Taps and the basket. Gradually the gap closed: 31-22, 32-24, 32-26, 34-30. Then Speed called time out.

Coach Rockwell, on his feet, talked to Soapy Smith. Soapy nodded his head and struggled out of his jacket. No longer did the other players nudge one another or make sly remarks when Soapy entered a game. The team had confidence in him now, and he had caught the liking of the crowd. His never-give-in, die-hard spirit and unrelenting hustle made him Coach Rockwell's first alternate for the starting five. Soapy had arrived!

Soapy dashed to the scorer's table, reported for Ryan Scott, and hurried into the huddle where he began talking earnestly to Speed. When play resumed, Speed and Red continued their cutting tactics, but now Taps faked to them and then passed back to Soapy who took shot after shot at the basket. He was hot too and within five minutes had scored the last ten points.

The Delford captain called time with the score Valley Falls 44, Delford 33. The Delford second-half defense had been completely demoralized by the shift in Valley Falls's tactics; Soapy hadn't even been guarded when he took his shots at the basket. "Just like takin' candy from a baby," he delightedly told Speed in the huddle.

When play resumed, Coach Rockwell's strategy repeatedly forced the Delford players into defensive errors. When they dropped back to stop Speed and Red, Taps passed out to Soapy on the side for his shot. When they played Soapy close, Speed and Red cut under the basket and resumed their first-half attack. The game turned into a blowout, and Coach Jenkins's bellowing could be heard all over the gym. The Rock was having a wonderful time! The final score: Valley Falls 54, Delford 38.

DOWN THE STRETCH

It wouldn't be long now! Next Friday night would complete the picture. Southern was scheduled to meet the Iron Men at Steeltown, and the tall Salem Sailors, in line for a tournament bid too, were the last team on the Big Reds' schedule.

What a race! Section Two hadn't seen anything like it in years. Three teams were going into their last game of the season, each with thirteen victories and three defeats. Maybe there would have to be a playoff game. That was up to Southern's players.

Speed flew down the snow-covered steps as if he were on skis. Chip followed as best he could. The Mustang didn't even sputter when Speed turned the key and stepped on the gas; nor did it groan when Chip, Taps, Soapy, and the Scott twins piled in with scrambling legs and arms. It was rarin' to go—and did, sliding and galloping as hard as it could for the Hilton home and the TV. Yes, five minutes to make the eleven o'clock sportscast. No Sugar Bowl for Chip tonight!

Up on the porch and into the family room they raced. Speed punched the remote control as the others ran to the refrigerator for food.

"Hello, sports fans. This is Channel 10 bringing you up-to-the-minute sports headlines. So, without further delay, let's turn to high school basketball and the state tournament hopefuls.

"Weston, last year's state champion, as you know, finished the season with only two defeats—both by Valley Falls. The Cardinals, defending their great and unforgettable record of last year, earned the position for their invitation last Wednesday to participate in this year's tournament. They're certain to be the top-seeded team.

"Here's a score that's just been received from Steel-town where a major upset occurred tonight—"

"Yes!" yelled Soapy.

"They did it! They did it!" screeched Red. "Oh, man!"

"Quiet," reminded Chip, "let's hear the rest of it."

"Yes—Southern defeated Steeltown tonight—yes—Southern. Final score: Southern 36, Steeltown 32. That was a heartbreaker for Steeltown. The Iron Men were in a three-way tie with Salem and Valley Falls. It was Steeltown's fourth defeat and ended their chances for this year's tournament.

"I'll have the details on that Salem-Falls game in just a minute now. That game Southern lost to Valley Falls last week was the tip-off. The Big Reds were lucky to win that one—by a single point.

"And here's the score you've been waiting for. There was another upset tonight—"

"Here it comes!" exulted Soapy.

"The other upset occurred at Valley Falls. The Big Reds, playing their best basketball in weeks, upset the Salem Sailors 59-58. The Sailors had won thirteen out of sixteen and their last seven in a row. The tallest team in the state met its match tonight when Soapy Smith, sub-stitute star of the Big Reds, won his second game of the year by making good on a free throw in the last second of the game."

"I'm a star! I'm a star!" Soapy was dancing. "I'm a star!"

"You're a dork! Be quiet or you'll see those stars," threatened Speed with a happy grin.

"Smith broke a 58-58 deadlock with one second—one little second—left to play. Yes, Soapy Smith not only broke that game wide open but broke the hearts of the Sailors, as well—for that shot of Smith's put Valley Falls in undisputed possession of the runner-up position of Section Two and landed the Big Reds in the tournament.

"The free-for-all starts next Friday afternoon at State. Weston and Valley Falls finished at the top of Section Two, one-two, and will represent their division for state honors. Each of the four sections will send two representatives to the tourney. You can catch the action right here on Channel 10."

"Can you imagine that—" began Soapy.

"Quiet a minute," Speed bellowed.

"So now the tournament lines up with Weston and Valley Falls from Section Two, Waterbury from Section One, with Rutledge and Seaburg from Section Four, followed by Bloomfield and Edgemont from Section Three. That's the way it lines up right now—only one place open. That's in Section One. Looks as if Coreyville might get that berth. We'll know about that tomorrow night."

Speed turned off the TV and fell back on the couch. "Man, oh, man!" he said. "Can you imagine those young guys beating the Steelers?"

"Look out for Southern next year," said Ryan Scott.

Soapy's prophesy had come true; Valley Falls was in the tournament as one of the best eight teams in the state. In a few minutes the Big Reds would be on their way.

Chip had been busy getting ready for the two-day stay in University. Just a short time ago, he had taken one last look at the trophy case and Valley Falls's first state championship ball—the one his dad had won. Maybe Speed and the guys could bring this year's ball back. Maybe *he* could help win one next year.

The team bus was purring in front of the gym steps. Standing around and talking was just about everyone

Chip could think of—Mike Rodriguez, Pat Sanders, Lefty Peters, Joe Kennedy, and Pete Williams—the papers were going to be well-represented—Ted Williams, Biggie Cohen, and even Brandon Thomas.

Pop Brown, dressed in a three-piece suit, nudged his way through the group. He waved a paper at Chip. "Here's the tournament pairings, Chipper, right here in the paper."

Everyone crowded around to look at the all-important brackets. Weston had been seeded number one, just as predicted. Waterbury had been seeded number two and had been paired with Valley Falls in the first round.

"We would draw them," someone said.

"We'll kill 'em!" said Soapy.

Pop passed the paper over to Chip, and each player studied the pairings carefully, mentally figuring the possible winners and the Big Reds' chances.

"Coreyville made it, didn't they?" Taps asked.

"Fill her in, Chip," urged Soapy. "Here, do it the easy way. Put Valley Falls right over there at the end—right there in the championship spot and then work backward." He grabbed a pencil and leaned over Chip's shoulder to write "Valley Falls" on the championship line. "That's a pretty good draw sheet now," he roared.

"Weston will beat Bloomfield easy," said Speed.

"You're right," agreed Red. "Boy, wouldn't I like to meet them in the finals and beat 'em again!"

"Seaburg's a sleeper team. We better watch 'em," said Speed.

"Seems to me you guys better worry about Waterbury," laughed Chip.

DOWN THE STRETCH

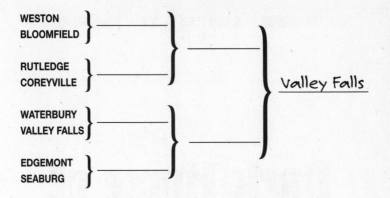

WESTON
BLOOMFIELD

RUTLEDGE
COREYVILLE

WATERBURY
VALLEY FALLS

EDGEMONT
SEABURG

Valley Falls

Dark Horse of the Tourney

CHIP USED his player's badge to gain entrance to the university gymnasium and trudged through the usual corridor crowd toward the court. Just inside the tunnel leading to the court, he paused in amazement—it was packed solid! He turned back and tried several other entrances with the same result; he couldn't even see the floor!

"How about that!" he muttered in disbelief. "Friday afternoon and standing room only! They love this game!" What would happen tomorrow when thousands of fans from all over the state began arriving for the Saturday afternoon games and evening finals? He searched around desperately. This was no good. Rutledge was the team to beat. He had to see this game.

He and Speed had been invited to State's spring athletic reception last year, and they had worked out on the court. That was it! Sure! He'd go down to the lower level where the teams dressed and then come up on the court by the team entrance.

Chip's idea had been a good one. Only a few officials and players were standing in the team entrance, and they were completely engrossed in the game. He edged a little closer to the long row of tables. Sportswriters from every paper in the state were busy taking notes, clicking away on their laptops, or wearing headsets and talking into microphones.

There was one vacant chair at the far end of the table. Before he realized it, he was on his way to that chair. Sitting down, he drew out several sheets of the State Hotel and Convention Center stationery and began writing furiously. He felt self-conscious, as if all those twelve or fifteen thousand people were watching him. Well, this was business.

Right after lunch, Coach Rockwell and Chet Stewart put the players to bed. The tension and emotional pressure of an eight-team tournament in which the champion would be forced to win three games in two days made it imperative that every ounce of each player's energy be conserved. After everyone was checked in, Chip had asked Coach Rockwell if he could watch the afternoon games.

Coach Rockwell smiled. "Sure, Chip," he said. "Rogers and Jerry Davis just left. Suppose you do a little scouting yourself, OK?"

Rutledge had been Chip's secret choice as the team to beat in the tournament. Larry Burger was bigger than Weston's Perry Fraling and had been burning up Section Four, scoring better than twenty points a game.

He glanced at the scoreboard. Rutledge was leading Coreyville, 16-12. His glance shifted over to the other side of the court to the scorer's table; tonight *he* would be down there at that table, and Speed and Taps and the rest of the team would be out on the floor.

Scribbling as he watched, Chip wrote notes: Rutledge uses a man-to-man defense . . . overshifts a little under the defensive basket . . . number 14 is too slow . . . turns his head too . . . Speed or Red could run him ragged. *Better put that down.* Use fast break . . . good too . . . it's all Burger . . . knows what he's doin' all right . . . bigger than Taps . . . stronger too . . . long arms . . . seems a little slow. . . maybe Taps can outmaneuver him.

Shoots right-handed only . . . Coreyville's center isn't big enough to hold him . . . right-handed hook shot. *Better write that down several times.* Right only.

"To beat Rutledge we have to do two things," Chip wrote. "One—stop their fast break; two—stop Burger!" He wrote that several times. Taps could do it; Taps would *have* to do it!

Coach Rockwell and Chet Stewart were seated in the lobby as Chip came hurrying in.

"All over?" queried Rockwell.

"Yes, sir! Weston and Rutledge! Rutledge looked awfully good, Coach!"

"Well, they're not in our bracket. We'll see how good they are when they meet Weston. We'll take them as they come, Chip."

"I've got some good notes on Rutledge anyway, Coach."

"Looking pretty far ahead, aren't you?"

"Guess so, Coach, but I think they're the team to beat!"

The newsstand girl's dimpled smile changed to a blank look as Chip asked for fifteen *Morning Telegrams.*

"Fifteen?"

"Yep, that's right—fifteen!"

The girl glanced curiously at the big VF on Chip's sweater and smiled again. "I get it," she said. "Did you win?"

"Sure did!"

"Going to win tonight?" The young woman wanted to keep the conversation going with the handsome athlete.

"Sure! That is, if we win this afternoon," Chip responded, oblivious to her interest.

He noted it was 9:15 by the lobby clock. The day's schedule called for a combination breakfast-lunch at eleven o'clock. That would be the team's only meal before the Seaburg game at two o'clock. Right after brunch, a team strategy meeting was scheduled to go over the Seaburg scouting notes, followed by a ten-minute walk and then back to bed.

After the victory last night, the players had a terrific meal: shrimp cocktail, soup, steak, roast potatoes, salad, and two big servings of ice cream. Coach Rockwell had taken charge of the after-dinner walk, had given them a brisk fifteen-minute hike, and then sent them to bed with instructions to stay there until 9:30 the next morning.

Chip went from room to room distributing the papers Coach Rockwell had bought, finally ending at the room he shared with Taps. He threw Browning a paper and opened his own to the sports section.

WESTON ADVANCES TO QUARTERFINALS
RUTLEDGE, SEABURG, VALLEY FALLS ALSO WIN

The Weston Cardinals, last year's undefeated state champions, defeated Bloomfield, Section Three pacesetter, in the opening game of the state tournament yesterday afternoon, 56-45. The Cardinals, led by their ace center, towering Perry Fraling, were in front all the way.

CHAMPIONSHIP BALL

Rutledge, seeded third, played possession basketball to topple a fighting Coreyville team by a score
of 63-40.

In the first game last night, Seaburg, runner-up to
Rutledge in Section Four, easily disposed of Edgemont, champions of Section Three, 66-44.

In the final game of the first day's play, Valley
Falls created a mild sensation by upsetting Waterbury,
Section One leader, by a score of 57-47. Waterbury's
2-3 zone was riddled by the precision shooting of
Valley Falls's Morris and Schwartz.

Today's semifinals call for the Weston-Rutledge
game at 11:00 A.M., followed by the Seaburg-Valley
Falls game at 2:00 P.M.

The third-place game will start at 7:00 P.M., with
the championship to be decided in the final tip-off
beginning at 8:30.

The Weston-Rutledge game this morning will pair
up two of the best centers in the state; Perry Fraling, the
Cardinal ace, will, for the first time this year, find himself up against a taller opponent. Larry Burger,
Rutledge's one-man team, stands six feet seven inches
and packs over two hundred pounds on his powerful
frame. Weston appears a slight favorite in this game
chiefly because of its tournament experience.

Seaburg is a strong favorite in the afternoon game.
Rutledge nosed out the Sea Bees by the narrow margin
of two points in the final game of Section Four's
schedule. Valley Falls has a great star in Morris, and its
upset victory over Waterbury stamps the Big Reds as
the dark horse team of this year's big show. However,
it is doubtful if the Big Reds can match the height of
the Sea Bees. Much depends upon Browning.

"I'll say it does," Chip muttered.

"What did you say?" Taps was nervous.

"It says here we're the dark horse of the tournament, the underdogs."

"That's good, isn't it? Anyhow, we've got a chance to win third place."

"A chance to win third place! Are you kidding? What do you mean, *third* place? We didn't come up here to win third place. We came here to win the *championship!*"

Anyone would have thought the squad of boys had been starved for a week. They tore into Coach Rockwell's team brunch as if it were their last meal. Their joking and laughter didn't indicate that they had to play an important basketball game at two o'clock either. But that was just what Coach Rockwell wanted—the complete absence of pregame worry and stress.

Finally, Rockwell and Chet Stewart came over to the table. "OK, boys. Everyone feel all right? Good! A ten-minute walk, Chet. Then right back here to the team room so we can go over those Seaburg notes."

Chip lingered behind, trying to catch Rockwell's eye. But it was wholly unnecessary—the coach spoke first.

"Chip, you'd better rush over there and scout the upcoming Rutledge-Weston game. *I've* got a hunch *your* hunch is the right one—Rutledge!"

CHAPTER 23

Eight Little Seconds

CHIP HEARD the band before he saw it. The familiar chords of the "Valley Falls Victory March" greeted the bus as it turned up the drive and came to a stop in front of the main steps of the university gym. It was exactly 1:00 P.M. As the players piled out of the bus, they were nearly blown off their feet as the red-and-white-garbed band members ended the song with a resounding blast. Principal Zimmerman had promised to send the band if the team won in the first round. "We'll be there Saturday!" And they were!

Valley Falls was proud of the one hundred talented boys and girls who had won state honors more often even than the athletic teams. The Big Reds school band was big-time!

"Hi ya, Speed."

"Hello, Pop, how they feelin'?"

EIGHT LITTLE SECONDS

"Hey! Soapy!"

"What ya say, Red?"

"Good luck, Rock!"

"How about a ticket, Ryan?"

"Knock 'em cold, gang!"

"Go Big Reds!"

They were surrounded by about everyone they knew, it seemed. Practically all of the Valley Falls residents had said that if the Big Reds won their first game, they'd be there to see them win the championship!

Coach Rockwell and Chet led the determined squad through the pressing crowd of friends, up the steps, and into the locker room. Even Soapy had no desire to trade remarks with some of his friendly hecklers. After the game, they'd talk. Now it was time to take care of business!

Chip, holding the scorebook, leaned against the wall of the locker room. Coach Rockwell reviewed the Seaburg scouting notes. "They're tall and they're good—but you're better! Use lots of bounce passes; keep the plane of your passing low—they'll intercept anything up in the air! But those tall kids don't like to bend over. Open 'em up! Don't jam up the center, Taps. I want you to move and keep moving! Ankle all right? Taped? Everyone feeling OK? All right then—go out there and win that game! Let's go!"

Coach Rockwell solemnly stretched out his hand, and everyone in the room rushed to join hands in the traditional sports circle that signifies team spirit and bonding together for a common cause. "You lead them out, Speed! Let's go, guys!"

The Big Reds broke toward the door as if blown by a giant wind, pushing, elbowing, shouting, and pounding one another. Chip followed with Soapy's familiar "We'll kill 'em! We'll kill 'em!" ringing in his ears.

The crowd on the steps had been big, but this one was ten times as large. The gap between the team and Chip widened, and he had no choice but to resign himself to inch-by-inch progress. He was surrounded by shrieking students, cackling men and women, packed like sardines—bantering, cheering, pushing, laughing. It seemed as if everyone had a hot dog and a drink . . . everyone but Chip.

Up ahead there was a roar of applause, cheers, and the thunder of a thousand Valley Falls fans as the Big Reds dashed onto the floor. Chip finally got through the big aisle. As he turned down the side of the court toward the scorer's table, he saw the Big Reds cheering squad of eight boys and eight girls in formation in front of the Valley Falls section. The fans watched mesmerized as the male cheerleaders lifted the girls high above their heads. The girls' red-and-white skirts twirled in the air as they executed perfect somersaults before landing gracefully on the floor in a V-formation. There was a brief silence and then the rafters shook.

> *"Y-E-A V-A-L-L-E-Y!*
> *Y-E-A F-A-L-L-S!*
> *GO BIG REDS!*
> *GO VALLEY FALLS!"*

Across the floor, the Seaburg stands came right back with a thundering cheer for the Sea Bees.

Chip looked up at the mezzanine and the two broadcasting boxes. Draped below one was a big banner with WTKO lettered on it. Below the next box was the WKMT banner. Stan Gomez and Smiley Harris were on the job. He could see them peering down at the crowd, and his thoughts leaped back to Valley Falls. He could imagine the telephone office this afternoon—bedlam! It would be worse tonight, he thought. Mom probably would have to work overtime, but she'd have the radio on. About everyone in Valley Falls who could not be at the game would be listening to Stan Gomez right now.

Almost every town has a Main Street. Main Street in Valley Falls was a Saturday-afternoon street. On any other day, it was fairly peaceful and quiet as people went about their workday routines. But on Saturday afternoon, it seemed that nearly every one of Valley Falls's citizens was there at one hour or another.

Not so today. Only a handful of people were seen along the entire business section. But countless radios and TVs were tuned in to broadcasts of the game.

"Three minutes to go now—Seaburg leading by seven points. There's a shot by Browning—he misses—Browning looks tired, folks. Sea Bees' ball now—they're coming down the court—taking their time—these boys play a careful game—over to Billings—back to O'Brien—to Warder—Seaburg's protecting that lead. There's a shot by Billings—it's good! No—no—that's wrong—he missed the basket—the light down at that north end is bad—too hard to see from here with that crowd behind the basket.

"Morris has the ball—two minutes to play—he's up to the ten-second line now—over to Schwartz—to Scott—don't ask me which one—over to the other one, the other Scott—he bounces the ball in to Browning—at the free-throw line—that Seaburg defense is something to see—Valley Falls can't get near the basket.

"Less than a minute to play now. Schwartz cuts by Browning and then drops back—Browning gives the redhead the ball—Schwartz shoots—it's good! Seaburg's lead is cut to five points now—time is running out— Seaburg is holding the ball—there's the horn!

"So—at the half, it's Seaburg 31, Valley Falls 25. And here's Randy White to review the first half of this semi-final game. Take it away, Randy."

Ten seconds before the horn ended the first half, Coach Rockwell had cleared the bench. Chet Stewart had waited at the side of the court and had ushered Browning, Morris, Schwartz, and the Scott twins directly to their assigned locker room. Each one of those fifteen intermission minutes was precious.

The Rock was talking.

"All right, pay attention now! That was a bad first half—I'm glad we've got that out of our system! You played right into their hands! They held the ball on the offense till they got a good shot. You drove in against their floating man-to-man defense and took bad shots!"

Coach Rockwell turned to the strategy board on the table and moved the five player pieces under one basket.

"How are you going to cut through a mob like that?" he demanded. "I waited for fifteen minutes before I saw a smart offensive play. What was the play, Speed?"

"Red's reverse offense play, Coach. Red passed to Taps, drove by him, and then fell back. Taps passed the ball back to Red, and he got an open shot. Their whole team fell back when the ball went in to the post and Red cut toward the basket."

"Right! I talked about their floating defense until I was blue in the face when I went over the scouting notes. You can't cut through it. You've got to drive 'em back and then take those easy shots.

EIGHT LITTLE SECONDS

"On the defense, you're letting them draw you out. You know their attack is all under the basket, so why lunge and dive? Make them come to you. Understand?

"All right, so much for that! Now, this half, I want you to play possession ball too. We'll give 'em a little of their own medicine. We're better passers, we're better shots, and our defense is just as good. I can't believe you're going to let Seaburg outsmart you.

"We'll keep driving in and driving 'em back, and then we'll pass the ball out to Schwartz and Speed. Then we'll follow in—Browning, Schwartz will follow in on every shot and tap or throw that ball back out to Ryan—if we get it—and then we'll start all over again. OK?

"We can take a chance on four men following in because they never run a fast break—*never* a fast break, get that?

"On the defense, we'll stop lunging—we'll wait. We'll let them make the first move. OK.

"Now, Ryan, you're in charge of the backcourt. You're the defensive quarterback. Don't get caught without help! Understand?

"Browning, Taps! You're the key to the attack. Don't try to dribble under the basket. Fake the shot, fake the pass, and then zip that ball back—hard—to Speed or Red. Understand?

"Now, Speed! I want you to take more time. You're hurrying your shots and you're not following through. There's no one near you; this is just like shooting in the Valley Falls gym unguarded. Soapy says, 'Just like taking candy from a baby'—if you do it right!

"And you, Schwartz. You start following through on your shots too. I want to see that shooting hand finish up pointing into the basket. Into the basket, you understand?

"All right. This is it! Let's go!"

CHAMPIONSHIP BALL

"One minute to play. Seaburg leading by four points—they're freezing the ball—the Falls boys are pressing Seaburg all over the court—it's a battle down there—Warder has the ball now—Morris is playing him close—Warder dribbles to the corner—he passes out to Carroll—Schwartz is right on top of him—he may foul if he's not careful—thirty seconds now—the crowd is pushing to get out on the floor—this game is almost over—twenty seconds—what a game!

"Billings has the ball—he's dribbling back along the sideline toward the ten-second line—Morris is swarming all over him—ten seconds! There's a whistle—can't see what it's all about—looks like it could be a foul on Morris. No!—it's Falls's ball out of bounds—Billings stepped on the sideline—the clock is stopped!

"Billings is still hanging onto the ball—he won't give it up—he's lost his head! He throws the ball up in the crowd—the referee has called a technical—I think—yes—it's a technical foul! He must have thought the game was over and started to celebrate. The clock is stopped—eight seconds to go—Morris is at the line now for two shots—listen to that crowd! Morris shoots—it's good! His second shot hits nothing but net!

"The referee is walking to the middle of the court—it's going to be Falls's ball for a throw-in at the division line. There's eight seconds to play—this game isn't over yet, anything can happen. Morris is standing on the sidelines—the referee hands him the ball. There's just eight little seconds to play—time isn't in until the ball is touched on the court. There it goes—Morris passes to Schwartz—back to Morris—in to Browning under the basket—he shoots—IT'S GOOD—IT'S GOOD! Tie game—46 all—we're headed into overtime! What a game!

EIGHT LITTLE SECONDS

"Folks, that's one for the books. Browning pivoted and shot the ball just before the horn sounded—but the ball was clearly in the air so the goal counts. After one minute we'll—wait a moment—

"There's something going on down there—the referee's signaled a pushing foul—it's definitely on the defense—he's handing the ball to Browning on the free-throw line. Browning was fouled during the shot. The basket was good—he's going to get one free throw—maybe there won't be that extra period after all! It's all up to Browning right now!

"Browning must be really nervous—he bounces the ball one, two, three times—he's looking up at the basket—he shoots—IT'S ON THE RIM—IT DROPS IN! Valley Falls wins, 47-46!"

Back in Valley Falls, a hysterical Petey Jackson was pounding John Schroeder on the back and shrieking at the top of his voice. The storeroom was crowded; it had been since the start of the game. Anyone could have walked off with the cash register and half the store, and no one would have noticed it—or much cared either!

"Hush, you confounded fool," growled Doc Jones. "Watch!"

"The Seaburg crowd is stunned, folks—just sitting in their seats in disbelief—Valley Falls fans are swarming all over the floor—the scoreboard shows Valley Falls 47, Seaburg 46. The Falls crowd has Browning and Morris up on their shoulders—listen to those Big Reds fans!

"This game will go down in tournament history, folks. You wouldn't believe it could happen—I still can't believe it. With almost ten seconds to go, Seaburg had the ball and a four-point lead—Seaburg would undoubtedly have won this game if Billings hadn't lost his head and caused a delay of the game—Billings's unfortunate error will be long remembered by the Seaburg fans—by Valley Falls fans too!"

CHAPTER 24

Most Valuable Player

ONE POINT behind and fifty seconds to play. Rutledge was trying to sit on the ball. Burger would break out from beneath the basket and leap high in the air to get the ball. Taps was trying desperately to leap with him and reach the ball but was missing each time.

Chip could almost read the thoughts racing through Taps's mind. He was trying to decide whether to risk overrunning Burger in order to tap the ball away. If Taps overran Burger and the big Rutledge center snared the ball in spite of Taps's effort, he would be able to freely move to the basket for an easy dunk or layup and put the game on ice! Taps was also at risk of fouling the big man.

There wasn't much time left. Speed was playing "sleeper," but this was a good team, and it didn't fall for his deception. Rutledge made few bad passes and kept the ball moving. Chip saw that Taps was still undecided about handling Burger. As Burger again drove out to meet the ball, Taps made a move to try for the interception, but his nerve failed him. He looked over to Chip. Their eyes met. Chip looked at the big clock—it was now or never! He rose to his feet and nodded his head with all his conviction. Taps nodded back.

Seconds later, Burger broke out for the pass again. But this time, Taps sped by him and leaped high in the air. His fingers barely touched the ball, but it was enough for Speed to dash in and make the steal. Chip looked at the clock—fifteen seconds to play!

Speed started a hard dribble for the basket but was shut down. He turned, faked a shot at the basket, and then hesitated. Chip knew what Speed was thinking. Speed was figuring percentages. Even with the clock running down, Speed wouldn't lose his head. He wanted the best marksman on the floor to have that ball for the all-important last shot. Soapy was standing over on the right side of the court, ready to follow in if Speed tried for the goal. Then Speed faked to Matt and threw the ball to Soapy.

"Take it, Soapy!" he yelled.

Soapy never hesitated. He let the ball fly straight for the basket. Chip, gripping the table for dear life, watched the flight of the ball. It was a little too hard . . . it might . . . yes . . . yes—but it *didn't*. The ball rebounded high in the air on the left side of the basket.

Speed followed the shot and as the ball started its descent, he leaped with perfect timing and made the recovery. It seemed as though he was surrounded by the entire Rutledge team, but he managed somehow to turn and twist in the air and throw the ball right back to Soapy. Chip's mind flew back to Sy Barrett's famous shot.

Soapy had hardly moved from his position. When the ball came flying back to him, he stood as if powerless to move. He heard players shouting.

"Shoot!"

"Who's got him?"

"Shoot!"

"Stop him!"

Soapy's opponent had turned away from him and followed the ball toward the basket for the rebound. Soapy was wide open—completely unguarded. Chip's frantic eyes darted to the clock—two seconds!

"Shoot!"

Then Soapy squeezed off the jump shot, and as the ball arched high in the air, the game clock hit 00:00 and the horn exploded. The ball was spinning toward the basket and every person in the gymnasium was on his feet, eyes glued to the flying sphere. Not a player on the floor moved as the ball *swished* through the net to make Valley Falls . . . STATE CHAMPIONS!

Chip dropped back in his chair, utterly exhausted—and he hadn't even played. He didn't even bother to mark the final score in the book. He sat completely still with his eyes glued on the scoreboard: Valley Falls 54, Rutledge 53.

Forever and ever, people in Valley Falls would talk about Soapy's shot—just as they had talked about Sy Barrett's. What a guy, that Soapy!

Speed grabbed the ball out of the hands of the indulgent referee and ran to help the other players get Coach Rockwell on their shoulders. The Valley Falls faithful had already elevated Soapy, and now he was triumphantly making a victory speech: "It was this way—"

They carried Rockwell and Soapy out to the center of the court where the state championship trophy was to be presented.

Chip was holding his precious scorebook as if it were made of solid gold. When the large golden trophy was presented, the team let Coach Rockwell scramble down but kept Soapy up in the air. Soapy liked it! He was throwing kisses to the crowd, patting himself on the chest, and talking a mile a minute. "You see, it was like this—"

When the team posed for the photographers, Coach Rockwell put his arm around Chip's shoulder, and Speed gripped him by the arm on the other side. Behind him a towering Taps rumpled his hair and shouted something. Chip had never been so happy in his whole life.

As soon as the pictures were finished, the players started through the crowd for their team room. Chip held the scorebook high and kept shouting the score, "Fifty-four to fifty-three! Fifty-four to fifty-three!"

Coach Rockwell was holding the big basketball-shaped trophy emblazoned STATE CHAMPIONS!

Across the floor barged the Big Reds, digging elbows, pushing shoulders, yelling hilariously. Speed was fighting his way through the crowd, his right hand pushing people aside while he clutched the championship ball under his left arm. Chip was carried along with the crowd and just managed to squeeze inside the locker room.

It was a madhouse! Players shouting, yelling, throwing towels, shoes, warm-ups, everything and anything they could get their hands on. Outside, the hall was filled with a throng of cheering friends and fans.

This was one night Coach Rockwell's "no visitors" rule was forgotten. Most of Chip's crowd was there, yelling and having the time of their lives. Here and there were a few photographers and reporters trying to get a word in edgewise or take a picture but having no success. Cheering friends and happy parents were smiling, patting backs, and wildly celebrating.

Coach Rockwell was standing on the table in the center of the room trying to get the team's attention. "Boys—" He paused and looked around. "Boys," he said when they had quieted, "we've got to make an important decision tonight—right now!" He held the championship ball up in the air.

"This is Valley Falls's first state championship ball in eight long years. You know the tradition—the championship ball is always given to the fellow who does the most to win it. We've got to decide who gets this ball. Here, Chet, mark down the votes. Who gets the—"

The sentence was never finished for the roar from Chip's teammates drowned out everything else: "Hilton! Chip! Chip Hilton!"

"GIVE IT TO CHIP!"

Chip heard the shouts, but the words didn't register. The next thing he knew, Speed was pushing him toward the table. Coach Rockwell, smiling and holding the championship ball, extended his other hand to hoist Chip beside him.

Chip tried to speak, but there just wasn't any room in his throat for words to get past something as big as a basketball that had lodged halfway between his heart and his mouth. It was surely going to suffocate him. What was this all about?

Slowly it sank in. This was no dream. The team and Coach were giving *him* the championship ball! Why? He wasn't even a player on the team! He hadn't played in a single game. *This* wasn't right—the ball belonged to Soapy—or Speed—or Taps! He tried to push the ball back, but Coach Rockwell's hands were like steel bands on his arms, holding him helpless.

As the wild cheering quieted, Coach Rockwell shook him gently and said, "Hilton, you worked harder than all of us put together to win this ball. There wouldn't have been a championship ball if it hadn't been for your spirit and devotion to our team. This is a championship ball for a real champion!"

There was a scramble of legs and arms as Speed and Soapy crowded on the table beside him. "How about a cheer?" they yelled. "Come on, guys, let's hear it!"

"Y-e-a H-i-l-t-o-n! YEA CHIP! CHIP HILTON!"

CHAPTER 25

His Father's Son

SLEEP WAS impossible. Chip had been awake long before his mother began bustling around in the kitchen. He joined her at the breakfast table, and they discussed the celebration of the evening before—the bonfire on the square and the impromptu parading down Main Street.

Later, pasting tournament clippings in his scrapbook, Chip's thoughts traveled back to the day he had argued with Speed, the day he had lost his head and thrown the book across the room. Those pages of clippings meant something after all.

The ringing of the doorbell jarred him back to the present, and he went into the hall. It was Doc Jones.

"Hi ya, Chip. I thought I'd drop over and shake your hand! Couldn't get near you last night at the celebration. Just wanted to congratulate you for winning the ball!"

"Doc, I don't feel right about that ball. I'm awfully proud of it, of course, and it means a lot to have it, but, well, I just don't deserve it."

"No?" Doc Jones shook a finger under Chip's nose. "Well, boy, let me tell you something about young people you don't know. Kids don't pretend when their hearts are concerned. They gave you that ball because they honestly believe you are entitled to it, and knowing all the things *I* do about your work with that team, I know that they were absolutely right!"

"Yes, but—"

"No buts! By the way, how's your leg?"

"Why, fine, Doc—I guess. I never think much about it now. Things have been too busy and exciting to give it any thought."

"Got your brace on now?"

"Yes, sir. Sure, Doc."

"Well, suppose we go in the family room and take it off. I'd like to take a look at that ankle."

Seated in the family room, Doc Jones and Chip let their conversation turn back to basketball. Finally, Jones stood up, shifting the brace from one hand to the other. "Well, I've got to go, Chipper. Drop up to the office sometime."

Chip followed him to the porch. Good old Doc.

"Wait! You forgot about the brace, Doc."

"Oh, so I did, so I did." Doc looked down at the brace in his hand. "It's been a pretty good one, hasn't it?"

"Sure has, Doc."

"Well, so long again, Chip." He started down the steps.

"But the brace, Doc."

"Oh—oh, yes. Well, I'll give it to someone who needs it, Chip."

"Someone who *needs*—Doc! Don't *I* still need it?"

"You?" Jones laughed. "I don't see what for."

"You mean I can walk without it, Doc?"

"Did pretty well just now!"

"And I can climb up stairs without it?"

"Sure! If you want to!"

"You mean, Doc, I can maybe *run* without it?"

"If I remember right, you used to be pretty fast."

"And—and—can I play baseball?"

"You always could!"

"You *really* mean it, Doc?"

"Did I ever fool you, Chipper?"

"Not that I know about! So long! Thanks, Doc!"

At the foot of the stairs he stopped. He *was* bewildered. He turned and dashed into the living room and grabbed the state championship ball from the table, singing enthusiastically to himself, "And when it *goes,* he'll be aglow—EE-YI, EE-YI, OH!"

Thoughts rushed madly through Chip's mind. *I'll take the ball over to the gym. Coach said he's gonna put it in the trophy case alongside Dad's! Hope he's there. Just gotta tell him the news, Gotta tell everybody. Gotta call Mom. She told me this would all pass.* "EE-YI, EE-YI, OH!"

Chip hurried toward school. As he turned the corner, he saw Coach Rockwell slowly ascending the steps to the gym. Quickening his pace, Chip darted forward and, without thinking, dashed up the steps.

Coach Rockwell heard him coming and stopped at the landing. "Why, Chip! How about your leg?"

"I can run, Coach! I don't have to wear that brace anymore! See? It's gone! Doc took it! He says my ankle is as strong as ever—I can even play baseball!"

CHAMPIONSHIP BALL

Chip looked up at the remaining steps . . . twenty-five, twenty-six, twenty-seven, twenty-eight, twenty-nine, thirty.

"Look, Coach!" With a mighty spring, he took the short flight three at a time.

Standing in front of the trophy case, Coach Rockwell and Chip gazed at two state championship balls—side by side. Chip remembered Coach Rockwell's words: "If your dad were in your shoes, he'd be right in there pitching, giving all he had for the team, whether he was the star, a sub on the bench, or the manager!"

All the worries and all the events of the past months came flooding back to him. Now it was all as clear as a picture. He could see and understand it all.

Speed, Taps, and Coach had planned all along to make him manager. From the very beginning Speed had needled him into fighting back, and Taps had put on an act for days on end with the pivot stuff.

Now, he reflected, he could understand why Taps had looked so bad when he was practicing with him and then looked so marvelous in the games. Chip had been hoodwinked all the way.

Chip wished he could put into words all the things he wanted so desperately to say to Coach and Speed and Taps and all the guys . . . what they meant to him . . . what the ball meant too.

And the steps, yes, those thousands of steps he had counted during the past four months. To earn that ball he would have crawled up every one of those steps . . . one by one . . . a million times! Nothing would ever have been important in his life if he hadn't whipped his self-pitying sob stuff and if he couldn't have been near the team, his friends, and the Rock.

HIS FATHER'S SON

Chip turned away from the trophy case to speak to Coach Rockwell, but he had disappeared. Alone in the gym foyer, a wave of gratitude swept over the boy as a mist stung his eyes and a painful lump gathered in his throat. Suddenly, he realized the months that had passed since that disheartening day when he had come home from the hospital would always remain the most important in his life.

Slowly, but with no sign of a limp, he walked over to one of the windows through which the March sun was streaming through the still-leafless trees. It was one of those balmy days in late winter when spring seems just around the corner despite the piles of dirty snow lining the sidewalks.

From across the street came a rhythmic thump, a unique sound produced only by a baseball thudding into a catcher's mitt. Two kids were playing catch in the driveway across the street. Chip executed an imaginary speedy tag on a runner sliding home and charged for the door and the flight of steps leading to the sidewalk below.

· · ·

Sports fans, don't miss *Strike Three!* It's the next book in this thrilling series of sports stories. Like his famous father, Chip Hilton starts out as a catcher on the Valley Falls baseball varsity. But when the Big Reds desperately need a pitcher, Chip proves he has what it takes to put the team in line for All-State honors.

You'll agree that *Strike Three!* is one of the most exciting baseball stories ever written.

The Coach Clair Bee and Chip Hilton Awards

THE COACH CLAIR BEE and CHIP HILTON AWARDS, like the Chip Hilton Sports series, place special emphasis on athletics, academics, integrity, and service.

The Coach Clair Bee Award honors the active Division One basketball coach who has made the most significant positive contributions to the game during the preceding year. The winner should reflect the character and professional qualities of Coach Clair Bee.

2000	Coach Jim Boeheim	Syracuse University
1999	Coach Jim O'Brien	Ohio State University
1998	Coach Jim Phelan	Mount St. Mary's College
1997	Coach Clem Haskins	University of Minnesota

"The two greatest influences in my becoming a college coach were my high school coach and reading the Chip Hilton Sports series."

    —Coach Jim Boeheim, Syracuse University

"I'm humbled to be linked with the name Clair Bee. The Clair Bee Award is one of my coaching highlights because it's about more than winning. The award is a reflection on everyone in our program, not just me."
   —Coach Jim O'Brien, Ohio State University

The Chip Hilton Award honors the Division One basketball player who best exemplifies the personal character traits personified by Clair Bee's fictional hero, Chip Hilton. Attributes include: athletic skill, academics, sportsmanship, service to the community, leadership, and personal integrity.

2000	Eduardo Najera	University of Oklahoma
1999	Tim Hill	Harvard University
1998	Hassan Booker	U.S. Naval Academy
1997	Tim Duncan	Wake Forest University

"This is probably the most prestigious award I've ever won, and I am extremely happy to have been considered with the other finalists."
   —Eduardo Najera, University of Oklahoma,
      Class of 2000

"I'm honored to be associated with the names Coach Clair Bee and Chip Hilton because they embody both academics and athletics."
   —Tim Hill, Harvard University, Class of 1999

more great releases from the

Chip Hilton ⭐ Sports Series

by Coach Clair Bee

The sports-loving boy, born out of the imagination of Clair Bee, is back! Clair Bee first began writing the Chip Hilton Series in 1948. During the next twenty years, over two million copies of the series were sold. Written in the tradition of the *Hardy Boys* mysteries, each book in this 23-volume series is a positive–themed tale of human relationships, good sportsmanship, and positive influences – things especially crucial to young boys in the 90s. Through this larger-than-life fictional character, countless young people have been exposed to stories that helped shape their lives.

WELCOME BACK, CHIP HILTON!

TOUCHDOWN PASS	**STRIKE THREE**	**CLUTCH HITTER**
0-8054-1686-2	0-8054-1816-4	0-8054-1817-2

available at fine bookstores everywhere